Heartland

❧

Breaking Free

Heartland

❧

Share every moment . . .

Heartland

❧

Breaking Free

by **Lauren Brooke**

SCHOLASTIC INC.

New York   Toronto   London   Auckland   Sydney
Mexico City   New Delhi   Hong Kong   Buenos Aires

With special thanks to Linda Chapman

No part of this publication may be reproduced in whole or in part, or stored in a retrieval system, or transmitted in any form or by any means, electronic, mechanical, photocopying, recording, or otherwise, without written permission of the publisher. For information regarding permission, write to Scholastic Inc., Attention: Permissions Department, 557 Broadway, New York, NY 10012.

Library of Congress Cataloging-in-Publication data available.

ISBN 0-439-13024-7

Heartland series created by Working Partners Ltd., London.

Copyright © 2000 by Working Partners Ltd.
Published by Scholastic Inc. All rights reserved.

SCHOLASTIC and associated logos are trademarks and/or registered trademarks of Scholastic Inc. HEARTLAND is a trademark and/or registered trademark of Working Partners Ltd.

24 23 22 21 20 19 18 17   6/0

Printed in the U.S.A.

First Scholastic printing, October 2000   40

For Pippa le Quesne — who has made Heartland
a very special place, with thanks and love.

Heartland

❧

Breaking Free

Chapter One

"Mom's not coming back, Pegasus," Amy said gently to the old gray horse. "She's never coming back." She knew that her words meant nothing to him, but she felt she had to say them — to try to explain.

In the weeks following the tragic accident, Pegasus had kept watch for Marion Fleming — standing expectantly at the door of his stall at Heartland, staring down the drive for hours until night eventually fell.

But now, in the past few days, Amy had noticed another change in her mother's favorite horse. Pegasus had become listless and quiet. Instead of looking out over the half door, he had taken to standing at the back of his stall, his head low, his eyes dull. It was as though he had given up looking for Mom and had lost all sense of hope.

1

Amy couldn't bear seeing him like this. She bent her face to his.

Pegasus snorted quietly and let his great head rest against her chest. Amy closed her eyes. Despite the sadness that hung over him, his huge presence still filled the stall — making her feel safe and at peace, just like it always had. It was the same presence that had once filled stadiums around the world and had made Pegasus and her father one of the most famous show-jumping partnerships ever known.

But that had been a long time ago; a time when she had lived in England and when her father still had been a part of her life; a time when Heartland hadn't even existed. Amy shook her head slightly. It was another person's life now.

Her thoughts were interrupted by the distant sound of a door opening. Giving Pegasus a kiss on his dark gray muzzle, Amy went to the half door of his stall. She could see the slim blond figure of her older sister, Lou, coming out of the weather-boarded farmhouse. Grandpa followed behind her, carrying a suitcase.

Amy opened the stall door and headed toward the house. "Are you leaving already, Grandpa?" she called.

Jack Bartlett stopped by the car and nodded. "Yes, honey. If I set off now, I can get there before dark."

Amy hurried to the car. "Give my love to Glen and

Sylvia." She put her arms around her grandpa's neck and hugged him hard, breathing in his familiar smell of old leather and soap.

"Don't forget to call when you get there," Lou said, giving Grandpa a kiss on the cheek.

Jack Bartlett looked from one sister to the other, his weathered face creasing in concern. "Are you sure you'll be OK? With all that's happened lately I'm not so sure I should go."

"We'll be fine," Lou said, her blue eyes meeting Amy's. "Won't we?"

"Of course we will," Amy replied. "And you can't *not* go, Grandpa. You know how much Glen and Sylvia look forward to seeing you."

Jack Bartlett didn't deny it. He always made a point of going to stay with his brother, Glen, and sister-in-law, Sylvia, for a month every fall. When Amy had been younger, she had gone with him to the Tennessee farm.

Grandpa was still looking worried. "Are you sure you can cope with the extra workload while I'm away?" he asked. "We're overstretched at the moment as it is."

"We've talked about this already, Grandpa," Lou said practically. "You know my friend Marnie's coming next week. She'll be able to help, and Ty's offered to put in some extra hours."

"Can we really afford that?" Jack Bartlett said. Amy

saw the wrinkles at the side of his eyes deepen as he thought about paying Ty, Heartland's stable hand, for the extra work.

"We'll find a way," Lou said, and then before he had the chance to speak again she interrupted him firmly. "Look, just go." She hugged him quickly and opened the car door.

"I'm starting to think you're trying to get rid of me," Grandpa said, throwing his suitcase into the trunk before getting into the car.

"You're absolutely right," Amy grinned. "We're planning wild parties while you're away, aren't we, Lou?"

Grandpa grinned back. "Sounds like fun. Maybe I'll stay after all." He saw Lou's expression. "OK, OK. I'm outta here!"

As he started the engine, Amy and Lou stepped back and waved frantically as he drove down the long, winding drive.

"Well," Lou said to Amy, watching the car disappear in a cloud of dust, "I guess it's just you and me now."

From inside the house came the sound of the telephone ringing. Lou's eyes lit up. "Maybe that's a new customer! I'll get it," she said, hurrying off.

Amy looked around the yard. To her left was the front stable block with its six stalls. White paint was peeling off the doors, and the wood around the door frames had been well chewed by the many different inhabitants over the years. Wisps of hay and straw were piling up under the water trough and scattered outside the stall doors. Amy sighed. The yard needed sweeping, and the mess around by the back barn was even worse.

She looked across the drive to the fields. Horses and ponies of all different colors and sizes grazed peacefully in the September sun. Amy's heart lifted at the sight. She knew that if it weren't for Heartland, most of those horses and ponies would have been put down — thanks to her mom's work they all had a second chance to live healthy and happy lives. Just seeing them looking so content made the hard work and long hours worthwhile.

Out of the fifteen horses that were currently at Heartland, twelve had been rescued from abuse and neglect; Amy and Ty were working to heal their mental scars so that they could be rehomed. Three horses were boarders whose owners had sent them to Heartland to have their behavioral problems cured — and then there was Pegasus. He had been Daddy's horse until the show-jumping accident that had led to Amy's father deserting his wife and family. After that, Pegasus had given his heart to Mom. Amy's eyes fell on the empty doorway of the end stall. Poor Pegasus — without Mom he seemed so lost.

The back door opened and Lou came out.

"Was it a new boarder?" Amy asked, but as she spoke she could tell from her sister's face what the answer was.

"No. Just a wrong number." Lou sighed, her eyes

scanning the yard. "We're going to have to fill those three stalls soon, you know, Amy. The boarders are our only source of regular income."

Amy nodded. The fees from the customers who sent their problem horses to Heartland helped pay for the rescue work.

"I just can't understand why there haven't been any more calls," Lou continued with a frown. "After Nick Halliwell started to recommend us we had a lot of interest. Now there's nothing."

"I could ring Nick and see if he knows of anyone who might need some help with their horses," Amy suggested. Nick Halliwell was a famous show jumper. Two months ago, Amy had cured one of his talented young horses of its fear of trailers. Since then Nick had been recommending Heartland to people he knew.

"It's worth a try," Lou agreed.

But when Amy phoned Nick Halliwell's barn, she discovered that he was out of the country, competing. "He won't be back for another three weeks," Nick's personal assistant explained.

Amy sighed as she put the phone down. "No luck," she said, turning to Lou, who was sitting at the kitchen table.

"It's just so weird," Lou frowned. "We haven't had one inquiry in more than a week now."

It *was* a bit strange, Amy admitted to herself. It *was*

unusual to not have any phone calls for an entire week. A feeling of unease ran through her, but she pushed it down. "Things will be OK," she said, trying to sound optimistic.

"I hope you're right," Lou replied. "We're going to run into difficulties if business doesn't pick up soon." She sighed and stood up. "Well, I guess we should go and get started on Mom's room."

The breath caught in Amy's throat. *Mom's room.* The words echoed in her head. Marion Fleming's bedroom had been untouched since the night she'd died, but now that Lou's friend Marnie Gordon was coming to stay for a few weeks, they needed the space. Lou had decided that the time had come to sort it out.

"It shouldn't take too long," Lou said as Amy followed her upstairs. "I thought we could divide the stuff into three piles: things to keep, things to donate to the Salvation Army, and things to throw away." She opened the door of the bedroom and walked in.

Amy stopped still in the doorway. She had tried to avoid the room since Mom's death, and now a sudden wave of emotion welled up inside her at the sight of the familiar objects and the faint smell of her mom's perfume. She struggled to control herself. It had been three months since the accident, and the unrelenting grief had subsided, but every so often the slightest thing would cause the pain and loss to come flooding back.

"OK," Lou said, walking over to a pile of cardboard boxes that she had brought in earlier. "Let's put the stuff we're keeping in this box and anything that's being thrown out or given away over there." She walked around the room and cleared her throat. "I guess we should start with the closet."

Feeling as if she was moving in a dream, Amy stepped into the room. The photographs of horses on the walls, the barn jacket on the back of the chair, the slightly crooked bedclothes, the hairbrush with a few strands of hair still caught in between the bristles — it was as if Mom were still alive, as if she were going to come walking into the room any second.

Lou opened the oak closet and for a moment even she was overcome by the row of familiar clothes hanging there. She reached out and touched the fabric of a skirt, and Amy saw her swallow. But when she spoke, her voice was still practical. "Well, shall we go through these first?" She hesitated again and then pulled out a couple of blouses. "Anything that's in OK condition can go to the Salvation Army, and I guess we should get rid of the rest."

"We can't throw out Mom's clothes," Amy said quickly. She caught her sister's eye.

Lou frowned. "But we have to make room for Marnie's stuff. Besides, Amy, it's something we need to do."

Amy couldn't bear the thought of getting rid of her

mother's clothes just yet. "Can't we just keep them somewhere else?" She walked to the closet and took out a pair of green riding breeches. Her stomach clenched. She could remember Mom wearing them just a few days before she died.

Lou gave way. "OK, for now," she said, sighing. "I'm sure there's room in the basement."

It didn't take long to pack away the clothes. Amy folded up breeches and shirts and sweaters from the shelves while Lou took down the few dressy outfits that Mom had owned and packed them quickly and methodically into boxes. When she reached the last item, she paused.

"Mom's jacket," she said almost in a whisper, looking at the navy riding jacket with its deep crimson lining.

Amy saw Lou's eyes suddenly fill with emotion and felt her own chest tighten. Mom had given up her own show-jumping career after the accident that twelve years before had injured Pegasus and Daddy so badly. Amy had only been three and didn't really remember anything about her life then. Her memories started after she and Mom had moved to northeastern Virginia to live with Grandpa. But she knew that Lou, eleven years old at the time of the accident, had many more memories of their life in England, memories that the jacket obviously brought flooding back.

Blinking quickly, Lou folded the jacket tenderly and

placed it on top of the other clothes. Then she started to clear out the bottom of the closet, the shoe boxes, the bits and pieces of makeup and jars of skin cream. "Look at this," she said, her voice tight.

Amy silently took out a jumble of shoes. Under them she found a wooden box. She opened it. "Photographs!" she said, looking at two faded blue-and-gold albums and several envelopes of loose photographs. She opened the pages of the first album. "Lou! It's you!" There was no mistaking the golden-haired toddler who looked out of almost every photograph, cornflower blue eyes wide and curious in her heart-shaped face.

Lou looked over Amy's shoulder. "Yeah, it is."

"And Daddy and Mom." There were photographs of their parents looking strangely young. Their father, tall with dark, curly hair. Mom, smiling up at him, small and slender with the same blue eyes and fair hair as Lou.

Amy turned the pages. There were pictures of their parents' show-jumping stable in England, the horses looking out from around a smart square courtyard with dark timber stables. There were pictures of their dad and mom riding in competitions, pictures of Mom's beautiful bay mare, Delilah, and Daddy on Pegasus. There were even pictures of Lou at just five years old, jumping around a course of jumps on a small pinto pony.

"That was Minnie," Lou said, kneeling down beside Amy with a smile. "Daddy bought her for me when I was three. Then when you were old enough to learn, you always wanted to ride her, so Dad bought me Nugget." She opened the second photograph album. "Hey, look! Here's when you were first born."

Amy looked at herself as a baby and leafed through the pages of the album until she found pictures of herself as a two-year-old — a skinny toddler with light brown hair and gray eyes. In almost every picture she was either by a horse or on a horse. She looked so different from Lou, more like her father.

Lou pointed to a picture of the whole family, all smiling, sitting on a beach by a huge sand castle. "That was when we went to Spain. You were just three, and I was eleven."

Amy turned the pages, eager to see more, but suddenly the photographs stopped. The rest of the book was blank. She looked at her sister.

"Daddy's accident," Lou said quietly.

Amy pulled out the envelopes and tipped the photographs onto the floor. They showed Amy and Mom with Grandpa at Heartland. Amy had grown by about a year, and Mom looked different, too, her face serious, her eyes quiet.

"That's me," Lou said, pulling out a photograph. It showed her standing outside the entrance of her English boarding school. She, too, was looking very serious, wearing a smart school uniform, schoolbag in hand.

Amy glanced at her sister. "Why didn't you come with us, Lou?" Mom had tried to explain it to her, but she had never been able to understand why Lou had wanted to stay in England at boarding school.

"Because I thought that Daddy would come back," Lou said.

"But Mom waited for months," Amy said, remembering Marion's words. "She said that after Daddy left she waited and waited but nothing happened." She frowned. "He deserted us, Lou."

Lou's eyes flashed. "He was trying to come to terms with never being able to ride competitively again. Showing was his life," she said fiercely. "He would have come back for us, but Mom just took off and left the country."

"Of course she did!" Amy exclaimed, memories filling her mind of the months when they'd first arrived in Virginia and Mom had been so distraught. "There's no way she could have stayed in England — it reminded her too much of him."

"If she *had* stayed in England, then maybe she'd have been there when he did come back, and then they could have gotten back together!" Lou said.

But he never did come back! Amy bit back the words. She knew that she had only been told her mom's side of the story, but she didn't see that there *was* another side. And she'd never understand how Lou could still support their father. Amy felt her mother did the only thing she could have done. After months of anxious waiting, Marion had sold all of the horses apart from Pegasus, who had been badly injured in the accident, and moved back to her family home in Virginia. There she concentrated on healing Pegasus and then started the equine sanctuary at Heartland. Through healing horses that had nowhere else to go, she gradually restored her own emotional well-being.

"I couldn't have lived here anyway," Lou said. "Mom would have wanted me to help and get involved, and I just couldn't handle being around horses after what had happened with Daddy."

Amy thought about the long years of growing up when she had hardly seen her sister and about the occasions when Lou had visited and there'd been arguments over her refusal to have anything to do with Mom's work. It was different now. Since Mom had died, Lou had rediscovered her love of horses. Amy fingered a photograph of Lou dressed in a long black university gown, taken on her graduation day in Oxford, England. Standing next to her were Mom and Amy herself.

Lou looked over her shoulder and smiled. "I couldn't believe you and Mom came all that way for my graduation."

"Mom was really proud when you were accepted at Oxford University," Amy said. "And when you called to say how well you'd done in your finals, she said that we *had* to be there to see you graduate. Not even Heartland was more important to her than that."

Lou looked surprised. "She actually said that?"

Amy nodded.

"I never knew," Lou said softly.

Amy squeezed her arm. "Mom really missed you, Lou. She was so glad when you got a job in New York."

Lou bit her lip. "But I still didn't come and visit much, did I? Oh, Amy, if only things had been different. . . ." Her voice trailed off. Suddenly she seemed to pull herself together. "It's pointless, thinking like this," she said briskly. "You can't live a life of regret. You have to move on." She started putting things into boxes again. "Come on. Let's finish up."

Amy put the photographs back in the envelope and put the albums carefully away. She carried the box over to the window. Mom's window, like the one in her own bedroom, looked out over the yard. Pegasus was still at the back of his stall, nowhere to be seen.

"I'm worried about Pegasus," Amy said, turning to help Lou, who was now clearing out the drawers of the dresser.

"You mentioned that he hasn't been himself lately," Lou said.

Amy nodded. "You know how he used to look out over the stall door for Mom after she died?"

"Like he was waiting for her to come home?" Lou said.

"Mmm," Amy replied. "Well, he's stopped doing it now. The last few days he's just been standing in the back of his stall, looking depressed. Something's wrong with him, Lou."

"I'm sure he'll be OK," Lou said, putting the lid on a box.

Amy glanced out the window, wishing she could feel so certain. "Mom meant everything to him. He must be really confused. Without a warning she's gone, and he doesn't understand why. I'm sure that's why he's so listless."

"Can you do anything to help?" Lou asked.

Amy thought about the herbal and other natural remedies that her mom had taught her how to use. She knew several different treatments for grief and loss. "I'll try," she replied. "I'll see what I can do."

Lou smiled at her reassuringly and opened another drawer. "I'm sure he'll perk up in a while."

They worked in silence for a few minutes. "I think we can throw these out," Lou said, opening the last drawer and pulling out a pile of letters and cards. She flicked through them quickly. "They're just old birthday cards and . . ." Suddenly she stopped. She pulled out an envelope from the pile.

"What is it?" Amy asked, seeing Lou's eyes widen.

Her sister didn't answer. Amy looked over Lou's shoulder. The letter was addressed to Marion at Heartland. "What is it?" Amy said again, not sure why Lou was looking at the letter so strangely.

"It was sent five years ago," said Lou, looking at the postmark.

"So?" Amy said.

Lou looked up, her face pale. "It's from Daddy," she said.

Chapter Two

❧

"It *can't* be!" Amy exclaimed, staring at the envelope in Lou's hands. "Mom never heard from him after he left."

"Well, it's his handwriting," said Lou. Amy saw her eyes glance at the address. "He sent it from England. *England!*" Lou swallowed. "He was there all along — I knew it!" She opened the top of the envelope, her fingers trembling, and took out a letter written on plain white paper.

"What does it say?" Amy demanded as Lou unfolded the letter and skimmed the contents.

There was a pause. "I was in England then," Lou whispered, her hand dropping to her knees. "Why didn't he contact me?"

"What does it say?" Amy repeated. Impatiently, she

snatched the letter from Lou. "Darling Marion," she read out loud. Her voice faded as she read on.

> Please write to me, just a note, a card — anything other than this silence. I know I did a truly dreadful thing, and I have blamed myself every day for seven long years. But please, please, find it in your heart to forgive me. We could start again together — just think how much we could do as a team. We were so good together once — weren't we? I know we could be again. I won't write any more now. Please tell the girls I love them and miss them. All I want is for us to be a family once again.
>
> I have never stopped loving you,
>
> Tim

Amy's arm seemed to go numb, and the letter fell to the floor. As Lou picked it up and started to read, thoughts began reeling through Amy's head. Mom had lied to her. Mom had told her that her father had never been in touch. And yet here was a letter from him, pleading for forgiveness, asking her if they could get back together.

She looked at Lou. Her sister's face was pale. "Why didn't he try to reach me?" she whispered. "I was the one who waited. *I* was there."

Amy shrugged helplessly. She couldn't believe it. Daddy had tried to persuade Mom to get back together with him. And what had been Mom's response? Had she written back? She pushed a hand through her hair, feeling her whole life and all it was based on disappearing like quicksand beneath her. Everything that she had thought she knew suddenly seemed less certain. What other things had Mom not told her? How should she feel about her father, now that she had read this letter?

"Do you mind if I keep it?" Lou's voice broke through Amy's thoughts. She was folding up the letter, her chin set at a determined angle.

Amy shook her head, hardly able to bring herself to speak. "No . . . I don't want it." She looked at her sister. The expression in Lou's eyes was unfathomable. "She never told me," she said to Lou.

"She never told either of us," Lou said. She put the envelope in the pocket of her shirt and then turned to the boxes, her voice suddenly brisk and practical again. "OK, let's go through the chest and then take some of this stuff downstairs." They continued to work in silence.

After clearing out Mom's bedroom, Amy left Lou to vacuum and dust and went outside to see to the horses. It was Ty's day off, and there was still plenty to do. Five stalls in the back barn needed cleaning, all the water buckets and hay nets needed refilling, and the horses still had to be brought in from the fields. Amy hurried around, using the chores as an excuse not to think about the letter. Just knowing that five years ago her father had sat down and written to Mom was weird enough without thinking about the content of the letter.

She set to work grooming and working the three boarded horses, Swallow, Charlie, and Whisper. She rode Charlie and Whisper in the schooling ring and then concentrated on Swallow. He was a bay gelding who had come to Heartland to have his fear of traffic cured. He'd been working well in the schooling ring that week, and Amy had planned to take him out on the roads for the first time that day. But with one thing and another, it looked as if he was going to have to wait. She glanced at her watch. There just wasn't time. She would have to put off working him on the roads until the next day. Maybe she and Ty could take a ride together when she got in from school.

As Amy led Swallow up to the exercise ring, she thought about how much she missed Ty on the rare occasions when he took his days off. He had started working part-time at Heartland when he was fifteen and then, a year later, had left school to train with Marion full-time. He had been amazing in the last few months since the accident. In fact, Amy wasn't sure how they would have coped without him. He worked tirelessly and knew as much about natural remedies and working with problem horses as she did.

At feed time, Lou came out to help her. "The yard is such a mess!" she said as they filled the last of the water buckets.

Amy looked around. The yard looked even worse than usual — loose handfuls of hay and straw littered the ground, and feed buckets were piled haphazardly outside stall doors.

"It's no big deal," Amy said. "We can clean everthing up tomorrow."

"You'll be at school," Lou reminded her.

"I'll do it before I go," Amy replied. As far as she was concerned, a few misplaced feed buckets didn't matter — what mattered was that the horses were exercised, watered, and fed. She brushed off her jeans. "I think I'll spend some time with Pegasus," she said.

Lou looked at her. "Have you done all your homework?"

"Almost." Amy saw Lou's face. "I just have a little more to do, that's all."

"You're sure?" Lou said suspiciously.

"Positive," Amy lied quickly.

She headed for the tack room where the medicine cabinet was. Her homework would have to wait. Finding something to help Pegasus was far more important. Lou went back into the house, leaving Amy to decide which aromatherapy oils to use. Selecting three different oils that could help treat depression, she carried them over to Pegasus's stall, where she noticed that the feed in his manger had hardly been touched.

Putting down the unopened bottles of oil, Amy started to gently massage the horse's head, making small, light circles with her fingers. It was a treatment called T-touch that her mom had taught her. Her fingers moved over his ears and down his face, sensing where her touch was needed. Gradually she felt him relax.

Giving him a kiss, Amy stopped massaging him and un-screwed the top of the first bottle, offering him the oil to smell. She watched Pegasus's reaction carefully. He put his ears back and turned his head away. She was sur-prised. It was neroli oil, the remedy that was most effective with horses suffering from sadness and loss. But Marion had always said that horses must be allowed to choose their own remedies, and so Amy accepted the gray horse's reaction and offered him the next bottle — yarrow. Again he turned his head away. Frowning slightly, she offered him the third bottle. Pegasus sniffed at it and then lifted his upper lip as if he were laughing. He reached for the bottle with his lips.

"No, you don't," Amy said, quickly closing her fingers around the bottle. The oil had to be diluted before it was used. She checked the label — bergamot oil. It was good for balancing and uplifting emotions and was a stimulant for the immune system. It wasn't necessarily an oil for helping to deal with grief. However, if that was what Pegasus had chosen, then that was what she would use.

She returned the bottles to the tack room and took a larger bottle of diluted oil back to Pegasus's stall. Putting a few drops on her hand, she started to massage his nostrils. "You've got to start getting better," she told him. "You can't stay depressed like this." She looked at his aging body. His once dappled coat was now snow-white, his ribs showed slightly. He sighed deeply and her heart ached for him. All her life Pegasus had been there. Whenever she was miserable and upset she would talk to him, and he would always listen and seem to under-stand. Now he was suffering and she had to try to help him — just as Mom had done all those years ago follow-ing the accident. "I'll make it better for you, Pegasus," she whispered. "I promise."

The next morning, Amy sat at the kitchen table try-ing to eat a muffin and do her math and history assign-ments at the same time. She had meant to finish them the night before, but almost as soon as she had sat down at her desk her eyes had closed, and she had fallen asleep on her books.

"Amy! I thought you said you were done with

your schoolwork!" Lou exclaimed, coming into the kitchen.

"I've just got a bit to finish here," Amy said defensively.

Lou looked at the half-written page. "A fairly large bit by the looks of it!" she said. "And the bus will be here in ten minutes. Oh, Amy, when will you . . ."

She was interrupted by Ty coming into the kitchen. "Hey, guys. What's up for today?" he asked, leaning against the door frame, his dark hair falling down over his face as he looked at Amy.

"I don't know," Amy said, scribbling another few sentences. "Swallow was really good yesterday, he's ready to go —" she was about to say *out on the road,* but she broke off as the second part of the history assignment caught her eye. "Help! Ty, do you know anything about revolutions in medicine in the late nineteenth century?"

"Sorry," Ty said. "Can't help you there. So Swallow's OK now? What about Charlie and Whisper?"

"Amy! You're going to miss the bus if you don't get a move on!" Lou insisted.

Amy swallowed the last piece of muffin and shoved her books into her backpack. "Just do what you want with them," she said quickly to Ty, her mind on her assignment. Maybe she could finish it on the bus. Matt and Soraya could help her.

"OK," Ty said as she rushed out past him. "Bye."

❧

Amy got to the end of the drive just in time to stop the bus. Seeing Soraya sitting near the back, she made her way there. "Hi!" she gasped, collapsing onto the seat beside her best friend. "How was your weekend?"

"Good," Soraya said, shifting in her seat to make more room. "How about yours?"

"Not great," Amy admitted. "And I still haven't finished that history assignment."

Soraya shook her head. "One day you're going to surprise me and actually do your homework on time." She rummaged in her bag. "Here. Take a look at mine."

"Thanks," Amy said gratefully, getting out her own book.

"So what was wrong with the weekend?" Soraya asked, as Amy found a pen.

"Oh, you know — just things." Amy looked up and saw Soraya's concerned brown eyes. "Pegasus isn't eating," she sighed. "We haven't had any calls about boarders for more than a week now. Grandpa's gone to Tennessee, which means extra work for Ty and me, and then yesterday when Lou and I cleaned out Mom's room, we found a letter that my dad had written to Mom five years ago."

"But I thought your mom hadn't heard from him since he left!" Soraya exclaimed in surprise.

"So did I," Amy replied. "And he said in the letter that he wanted to get back together with her."

"Get out of here!" Soraya gasped. "Are you OK?" she asked curiously.

Amy wished she could find the right words to express the confusion she had been feeling since reading the letter. "I'm not sure," she said at last. She paused. "I always thought that he'd just abandoned us without another thought, but that's not true and — and —"

"And it makes you feel different about him?" Soraya said.

Amy nodded. "I think so. And Mom, too," she added, glancing quickly at her friend.

Soraya squeezed her hand. She didn't say anything — she didn't need to. Amy knew that she understood. Suddenly, not wanting to think about the letter anymore, she looked down at the history worksheet. "Did you understand the second part of this?" she asked.

Soraya accepted the change of subject. "Yeah. Take a look."

Amy read through Soraya's notes and quickly started scribbling her own answer.

"Have you got anything else to do?" Soraya asked.

"Yeah, math," Amy replied. "But I was sort of hoping that Matt might help me with that."

"I'm sure he will," Soraya said, giving her a sideways grin. "Matt would do *anything* for you, Amy."

Amy feigned innocence. "I don't know what you mean."

"Sure you don't," Soraya said sarcastically. She shook her head. "Poor Matt. Every other girl in the school would jump at the chance to date him, and he goes and decides that he likes you."

Amy grinned and bent her head over her work.

A few stops later, Matt Trewin got on the bus. He sat down in the seat in front of them and grinned. "Still doing your homework, Amy?" he said. "How unusual."

"I need help, Matt," Amy pleaded, looking up from the last line of the history assignment. "I've still got the math homework to do."

"OK," Matt sighed. "Where is it?"

Amy handed him her book. He scanned down the page. "This doesn't look too bad," he commented. Matt was a straight-A student who wanted to be a doctor. Amy's report cards were more likely to be covered with Cs and comments like "has ability and could achieve more than her current grades suggest." She didn't mind school — it was just that studying always came second to Heartland and the horses.

By the time the bus reached Jefferson High, both of her weekend assignments were finished. "Thanks, Matt," Amy said as they got off the bus and headed for their lockers.

Matt gave a wry smile. "Anytime." He left Amy and

Soraya to go to his own locker around the corner from theirs.

"Oh, no," Soraya said in a low voice, her eyes suddenly fixing on a point over Amy's left shoulder. "Look who's coming."

Amy glanced around. Walking toward them were three girls, all with meticulously applied makeup and shiny, perfectly cut hair. They all looked somewhat alike, dressed in the very latest designer labels. The girl in the center paused. Seeing Amy and Soraya, she raised her carefully plucked eyebrows into an arch and walked over, her pale blond hair bouncing on her shoulders. Amy couldn't help but think of a shampoo commercial.

"Well, hello, Amy," the girl said, stopping in front of her and tilting her head to one side.

"Hi, Ashley," Amy acknowledged her stonily.

"So how's business at . . ." Ashley paused. "Heartland?" The way she said it made Heartland sound like some small, run-down, four-stall affair.

"Fine," Amy said, lifting her chin defiantly. "In fact, we're very busy."

Ashley's lips curved into a smile. "That's not what *I've* heard." Ashley Grant's family owned an upscale riding stable called Green Briar. Her mom, Val Grant, specialized in producing push-button horses and ponies for hunter jumping, but she also offered a service curing problem horses. Her methods, however, were very different from those used at Heartland.

Amy frowned. "What do you mean?"

Ashley looked around at her two friends, Brittany and Jade, who had moved up to join her. "Should I tell her?" It wasn't a question that required an answer. They smiled at one another.

Amy stepped forward, refusing to be intimidated. "Tell me what?" She felt Soraya move closer to her and put a hand on her arm. Soraya hated confrontations, but Amy's anger was rising swiftly. "What are you talking about, Ashley?" she demanded.

"Oh, just that people are saying that Heartland's days are numbered," Ashley said. Her voice was airy, but her green eyes never left Amy's face. "And that with your mom gone there isn't anyone who can cure the horses."

"But that's not true!" Amy burst out indignantly.

Ashley laughed. "Come on, Amy. There's you, your sister from New York, and Ty. You can't believe people are still going to bring valuable horses to Heartland." She tossed her hair back. "Come on, get real."

"They are!" Amy cried. From the corner of her eye she saw Matt come up beside her. "They'll still come. How would you even know, Ashley?"

"Oh, I've heard the rumors," Ashley said. "They're going around like wildfire. You might as well face it,

Amy. You should sell Heartland. Daddy would buy the land from you." A catlike smile curved up her lips. "After all, our business is doing just great. *Our* barn has never been so full." She smiled at Matt. "Oh, hi, Matt." And with that she turned and walked away.

Amy made a move to follow her.

"Leave it, Amy," Matt said, grabbing her arm. "You know what Ashley's like. She's just doing it to get to you."

"And she's succeeding," Soraya said. "Just ignore her."

But Ashley's words had hit a raw nerve. Amy stared down the hallway. What if people *were* staying away from Heartland because they doubted if it had a future without Mom? They needed the chance to work with new horses to prove that she and Ty were good enough to continue her mom's work. If the boarders stopped coming, if there were no problem horses to cure, then what would happen to Heartland?

☙

As soon as Amy got back to Heartland that afternoon, she went to find Lou to tell her what Ashley Grant had said. Lou was sitting at the kitchen table writing an address on an envelope. She jumped guiltily as Amy came in and quickly slipped the envelope under a pile of papers.

"What was that?" Amy asked.

Lou seemed to hesitate for a moment, and then she shook her head. "Oh, just a bill," she said. She stood up and quickly started to clear her papers away. "So . . . how was school?"

Forgetting about the letter, Amy launched into a tirade about Ashley.

Lou listened intently. "So she says that people have been staying away on purpose?"

Amy nodded. "If it's true, what are we going to do? We can't have people believing that we can't cure horses anymore."

"Hmm," Lou said, frowning. "Well, we'll just have to come up with something."

The kitchen door opened and Ty came in. "Hey," he said. "Can I get your help?"

"Sure." Amy hurried upstairs to get changed. It took her less than a minute to pull on her work jeans and a T-shirt. Ty waited for her in the kitchen. "How much else is there to do?" she said, slipping on her boots.

"A good bit." Amy noticed that Ty's normally calm face looked unnerved. "I haven't groomed anyone yet, and three still need working. It hit me today just how much your grandpa normally does around here."

"It should be easier when Marnie arrives," Lou said. "She's coming on Saturday and she wants to help. She used to ride when she was a kid."

Ty nodded. "And having one horse less will help — but not with money, I guess," he added, glancing at Lou.

"One horse less?" Amy said in surprise, wondering what he meant.

"Swallow went home," Lou said. "His owner, Mrs. Roche, called this morning and asked if he was ready. She picked him up a couple of hours ago." She must have seen the confusion on Amy's face. "You said he was OK to go," she continued uncertainly. "This morning when Ty asked you, you said he was ready."

"No, I didn't!" Amy exclaimed, staring at her. Suddenly she remembered the half-finished conversation they'd had that morning. Her hand flew to her mouth. "I meant that he was ready to start going out on the roads, *not* ready to go home!"

Lou stared. "So he's not safe on the roads yet?"

"Of course he's not!" Amy cried, jumping to her feet in horror. "I haven't ridden him on them at all. What are we going to do?" She saw the look of shock on Lou's face and swung around to Ty. "Ty!" she exclaimed. "How could you let Swallow leave? You must have *known* he wasn't ready."

"But you said he was," Ty replied. "I guessed you'd worked him over the weekend."

Amy almost stamped her foot in frustration and worry. "I didn't have time!"

"Listen," Lou broke in quickly. "Let's just call Mrs.

Roche right now and explain." She ran to the phone. "Quick, find me the number."

Amy grabbed the client book and started to leaf frantically through it. What if Mrs. Roche had taken Swallow out on the roads? He was better than he had been but nowhere near cured. *Anything* could have happened.

"Here it is!" she cried, holding the book up.

But just then they heard the sound of car tires crunching to a halt on the gravel outside. Amy swung around and looked out of the kitchen window. "Oh, no!" she gasped, seeing a well-built, red-faced woman get out of the car. "It's Mrs. Roche, and she looks really mad!"

Chapter Three

Amy, Lou, and Ty hurried to the door. "Mrs. Roche," Lou began, "I was just about to telephone you, there's been a —" She didn't have a chance to finish. Mrs. Roche bore down on her.

"I want a word with you, Louise Fleming!" she demanded, her eyes furious.

"Mrs. Roche," Lou said quickly, "if you'll just give me a chance to explain."

But Mrs. Roche seemed in no mood to listen to explanations. "I picked up Swallow this afternoon because I was assured that he was cured of his fear of traffic. I took him out on the road as soon as I got home, only to be almost thrown under a bus. That may be your idea of a cured horse, but it's certainly not mine!"

"Mrs. Roche, you don't understand —" Lou began, but once again she was interrupted.

"I understand perfectly!" Mrs. Roche snapped. Amy could see the veins standing out on her forehead. "You've been making a living by trading on your mother's reputation without having the experience to deal with the problems you promise to cure."

"That's not fair!" Amy burst out. "It was a mistake! Swallow should never have left. We were about to call you."

"Amy's right," Lou said. "We're very sorry. If you'll just bring Swallow back we'll continue his treatment free of charge." She tried smiling at Mrs. Roche, but the woman was obviously too worked up for it to have any effect.

"Bring him back!" she exclaimed. "No way! I'm going to take him somewhere where they know about horses." She stalked off toward her car. "And you'd better watch out for yourselves," she shouted over her shoulder as she yanked open the car door. "I'm not going to keep quiet about this, and once I've spread the word you can say good-bye to anyone bringing their horses here anymore!"

"But, Mrs. Roche —" Lou cried.

The angry woman slammed her car into reverse and, revving the engine, turned around in a shower of gravel and disappeared down the drive.

Lou put her head in her hands. "Oh, this is not good!" she groaned.

"What are we going to do?" Amy cried.

"There isn't much we can do," Lou said, looking up. "We just have to accept it. I'll write her a letter of apology, of course. I could try to call her, but I doubt it'll change her mind. I just can't believe it — this is the last thing we needed."

Amy bit back her anger as she saw her sister's shoulders sag. "Don't worry, Lou," she said quickly. "It was just one customer."

"I'm really sorry, Lou," Ty said, pushing a hand through his dark hair. "I should have waited."

Amy shot a look at him — frustration at the stupidity of the situation and worry about what it could mean for Heartland flashing hotly in her eyes. *Of course he should have waited.* "I can't believe you let Swallow go!" she said accusingly.

She saw Ty's face stiffen.

"Oh, come on, it's not Ty's fault, Amy," Lou spoke up quickly. "I was the one who spoke to Mrs. Roche on the phone. And this morning you did say that Swallow was ready."

But Amy couldn't help herself. "You knew Swallow wasn't ready. Why didn't you think it through?" she cried to Ty. "You've worked here long enough!"

As soon as the words came out Amy wanted to grab them back. They had made Ty sound like he was just a hired hand. She made a move toward him, but he was already turning away from her, his mouth clenched.

"I'll be in the back barn if you need me," he said, his voice flat.

"Ty —" Amy's heart sank as she watched him leave. *What had she done?*

With her mind immersed in Heartland's financial problems again, Lou hadn't noticed what had just happened. She sighed. "Look, we can't just stand around wishing Swallow was still here. We need to think about what we can do to make things better. Let's go inside, make some tea, and talk about it."

"I'll just be a minute," Amy said. Leaving her sister to go into the farmhouse, she hurried after Ty.

She caught up with him by the tack room. "Ty, I'm sorry," she blurted out, putting a hand on his arm. "I shouldn't have shouted at you like that."

Ty's eyes were expressionless. "I'll live."

"But I didn't mean what I said," Amy said quickly. "I really didn't. I was just upset. I'm sorry." She waited, expecting him to smile his familiar grin at her, tell her that all was forgiven. But he didn't — he just shrugged.

"Whatever."

An awkward silence hung between them. Amy suddenly became conscious that she was still holding on to his arm. She loosened her grip and let her hand fall to her side.

"I'll be in the barn grooming Jasmine," Ty said flatly. With that he turned and continued to the back barn.

Amy stared after him in confusion. She had lost her temper with him before, but usually he accepted her apology. He knew what she was like. She said things she didn't mean when she was upset. So why was this time different? Maybe it was because she had never treated him like a hired hand before, like someone who was just paid to do a job. Feeling uncomfortable, she returned to the house.

Lou was sitting at the kitchen table, making some notes on a piece of scrap paper.

"What are we going to do, Lou?" Amy said, sitting down next to her.

Lou looked up. "If people are staying away because they think we aren't experienced enough, then having Mrs. Roche going around telling her story will only make things worse," she said. "However, what happened can't be undone, so I guess we should just try to weather the storm and prove them wrong. But I think we are going to have to make some changes."

"What kind of changes?" Amy asked doubtfully. Lou, with her practical business mind, had tried to suggest alterations to the running of Heartland before, but Amy had fought against them. She wanted things to stay like they were when her mother was alive. *Still,* Amy reminded herself, thinking about the success of the fundraising dance that her sister had organized that summer, *some of Lou's ideas worked.*

"Well, first of all I would suggest that we need to make the place look more professional," Lou said. She must have seen the confusion on Amy's face. "Come on, Amy, admit it — the place is a mess. There's hay and straw all over the yard, pitchforks and rakes just thrown in a corner, and the manure pile seems to have a life of its own! It doesn't give a good impression to clients who come and look around."

"It's only because Grandpa is away," Amy said. "Ty and I are just so busy with everything else."

"OK, I agree it's worse at the moment," Lou said. "But even when Grandpa's here the place never looks as neat as it should." She shook her head. "I think we need to give the place a makeover—repaint the stall doors, fix the fences, organize the tack room, and then make an effort to keep everything tidy."

Amy frowned. She liked the yard the way it was. But after the dance she had promised to listen to Lou's ideas. "I guess," she said, rather reluctantly.

"Great!" Lou said. "We'll start this weekend. Marnie can pitch in. Of course, having a clean yard isn't much use if we don't have clients to come and see it, so I think we should consider advertising." She turned to Amy. "You remember my idea about the brochure? Well, I'm going to work on that. Maybe it will bring in a few more boarders." Her face brightened. "If we get enough business we might be able to hire another stable hand. Just part-time — but it would help."

"It would have to be the right person, though," Amy said quickly. "Someone who's into alternative therapies and our way of doing things." As far as Amy was concerned, it would be out of the question to employ someone at Heartland who didn't believe in their mom's ideals.

"Of course," Lou said, sounding surprised. "But I'm sure that won't be a problem." Picking up her pen, she started scribbling a few more notes.

Amy frowned slightly. She had a feeling that finding the right person to work at Heartland wouldn't be as easy as Lou thought. A lot of people in the horse world were traditionalists who dismissed people who used alternative methods as crazy faith healers. She sighed. Right now, however, the problem wasn't about finding someone else to employ, it was about finding some new customers and managing all the work with just her and Ty. She stood up. "I'd better go and help outside," she said.

Amy headed up the yard, wondering whether Ty had forgiven her yet. She found him in the feed room making up the evening hay nets.

"Hi!" she said, looking hopefully at his face.

Ty nodded a brief greeting and then bent his head over the hay again.

Amy hesitated uncomfortably by the door. He was obviously still not over it. She wondered what to do. Finally she picked up a hay net and started to fill it. "Lou's been coming up with some ideas to help us get more customers," she said. Ty didn't respond. Amy persevered. "She's going to put together a brochure and drop it off at all the feed merchants and tack stores and places like that." She was aware that she was talking faster than normal, her voice unnaturally high. Ty continued to shake out the flakes of hay and stuff them into a net, his head bent. "She also thought that we could straighten up the yard a bit. She thinks it's a mess." She grinned, attempting a joke. "How can she possibly think that?"

Ty looked up at her, his mouth set in an angry line. "I've been busy," he said. "There are sixteen horses here and only so many hours in the day. I'll clean up after I'm done with the other stuff."

"Ty, I didn't mean — I wasn't criticizing you," Amy stammered. "Anyway, *I'm* usually the one who makes all the mess!"

Ty dumped the hay net he had been filling in the pile with the others. "OK. I'll go and start sweeping now," he said.

"Ty!" Amy exclaimed as he brushed past her.

For a brief moment she hesitated. Should she just let him go? But she couldn't. "Wait!" she said, leaping after him.

Ty stopped, his back still turned to her.

"I'm sorry." The words tumbled out of Amy. "I didn't mean what I said earlier. I really didn't. I should have talked to you about Swallow this morning, but I was thinking about my homework." She caught his arm. "Please . . . I don't want us to argue. You're too important to me." She saw Ty's shoulders stiffen and realized what she had just said. "Too important to Heartland," she stammered, adjusting her words.

Ty turned and looked at her. Amy hastily let go of his arm and tried to hide her confusion by laughing awkwardly. "I can't seem to keep my hands off you today."

Ty's lips flickered in a faint grin. "I seem to have that affect on girls."

Amy felt a rush of relief as she realized that he had forgiven her. "Whatever, in your dreams!" she responded. She saw Ty's face relax. "I really am sorry about before," she said more quietly. "It was my fault. I wasn't paying attention this morning. I had no idea that I made it sound like Swallow was OK."

"It's OK," Ty said. He shrugged and walked back to the hay nets with her. "It's not all your fault. I guess I overreacted. It's just difficult." He glanced at her. "You know, this place, now that your mom isn't here."

Amy nodded. It was a huge responsibility. She felt it as well.

"Hey, don't look like that," Ty said softly. "We'll make it."

She lifted her eyes to his. "We have to," she whispered, seeing in Ty's eyes the same mixture of uncertainty, hope, and fear that she felt in her own heart.

At feed time Amy brought Pegasus in from his field. He walked slowly up the drive beside her, his seventeenhand frame looking gaunt, his ears flopping listlessly. The bergamot oil appeared to not be of much help. However, Amy knew she couldn't expect a miracle cure. Natural remedies often took time to work. She got the bottle and offered him a few drops on the back of her hand.

Pegasus licked them off, his tongue rasping against Amy's skin. She looked at his ribs, showing more clearly than ever, and bit her lip.

"I think I'll give Pegasus a bran mash," she said, going to the feed room, where Ty was scooping grain into yellow buckets. "I need to tempt him into eating something."

"Try adding a banana and some honey to it," Ty suggested. "They're good for energy."

Amy nodded. However, even with the addition of

some dried mint powder that Pegasus normally adored, he only picked at the hot mash. She stroked him as he rested his muzzle on the manger. The hollows under his ears were pronounced, and his eyes looked sunken. "What am I going to do with you, Pegasus?" she said softly.

He snorted. Putting an arm around his neck, she leaned her cheek against his rough mane. She couldn't bear seeing him so depressed. Leaving the stall, she went to find Ty.

"I'm going to call Scott," she said.

"Yeah, I would," Ty agreed.

Amy went down to the house. Scott Trewin, her friend Matt's brother, was the local equine vet. He was a young doctor who believed in using alternative therapies alongside conventional medicine. Through sharing an interest in Marion's work, he had become good friends with her before she died. Amy phoned him at his office. He asked a few questions and said he'd stop by later to check on Pegasus.

"It's not urgent, Scott," Amy said to him, not wanting to cut into his evening. "We're just a bit worried."

"I'll come over tonight. It's not a problem," Scott said, his deep voice reassuring. "I haven't got anything else on, and I'll be passing your place anyway."

"Thanks," Amy said gratefully.

❧

At six thirty, Scott's battered Jeep came bumping up Heartland's drive. "So Pegasus hasn't been eating?" he asked, taking his black bag out of the car and walking toward the barn with Amy. Scott was fair and tall, with a broad-shouldered frame.

"No," Amy replied. "And he's been very quiet. I think he really misses Mom."

In the stall, Scott patted the old gray horse and then listened to Pegasus's heart and breathing before taking his temperature.

"Well, there doesn't seem to be anything obviously wrong," he said at last. "Although he's lost some weight. It could be a virus — have any of the other horses shown similar signs?"

Amy shook her head.

"I'll take a blood test," Scott said, taking out a syringe from his bag.

Amy watched the deep red blood filling up the tube. "Do you think it could be because of Mom?"

Scott considered the question as he removed the needle. "Maybe. Some people would disagree with me, but I think horses can feel grief and loneliness when they lose a close companion — whether it's another horse or a human. Pegasus's symptoms are pretty general. That could be a sign it's emotional — but these symptoms could also be from a physical illness like a virus or possibly something more serious."

"Something more serious?" Amy echoed in alarm. She hadn't considered the possibility of Pegasus being really ill.

"I'm sure it's nothing to worry about," Scott said. "He'll probably perk up in a day or two."

Amy patted Pegasus. "I hope so."

Just then Lou looked over the stall door. "Hi, Scott."

"Hey," Scott said, his eyes lighting up. "How's it going?"

"Fine," Lou said. "Have you found anything wrong with Pegasus?"

"Nothing obvious," Scott replied. He repeated what he had told Amy and then packed his things away in his bag. "Well, I guess I'd better be off," he said, straightening up.

Lou opened the stall door for him. "Would you . . . would you like some coffee?" Her voice, usually so confident, caught hesitantly.

Amy looked at her sister and saw a faint blush creeping along Lou's cheekbones.

"Yeah," Scott said with a smile. "That would be great." He walked out of the stall and then, suddenly seeming to remember that Amy was there, he turned to her. "You coming, Amy?"

"I think I'll stay with Pegasus a while," Amy said. She watched as Lou and Scott walked to the house together, a thought suddenly forming in her brain. What if Lou and Scott liked each other? Until recently Lou had been going out with Carl Anderson, a guy she knew from Manhattan. But that was over now. Amy put her arms around Pegasus's neck. "They'd be just perfect together, wouldn't they?" she said to the old, gray horse.

Pegasus lifted his head as though nodding. Amy smiled. She knew it was only because a passing fly had happened to settle on his muzzle, but it seemed he understood.

"I love you," she whispered, kissing the side of his face.

Pegasus snorted softly in reply.

Chapter Four

❧

The next morning when Amy came into the house to get changed for school, she found Lou putting the phone down, her face worried.

"That was Laura Greene," she told Amy.

"Whisper's owner?" Amy said.

Lou nodded. Whisper was one of the two remaining livery horses. "She wants to take him away. She's coming with her trailer this afternoon."

"But why?" Amy demanded. "Things are going really well." Whisper had come to Heartland to be gently introduced to being ridden. After several weeks of carefully building up his confidence and trust, Amy and Ty had decided to get on him for the first time that weekend.

"She's been talking to Mrs. Roche," Lou said. "Guess where she's taking him?"

Amy knew from Lou's face what the answer would be. "Not Green Briar?" she said. Lou nodded. "But that's not fair!" Amy exclaimed. "They'll get all the credit, and we'll have done all the work."

"I know," Lou sighed. "But there's not much we can do."

Seething with rage at the unfairness of it all, Amy marched up the stairs. It was bad enough that Swallow left, but now Whisper, too. And Green Briar would get all the thanks, all the recognition.

❧

Her frustration flared up again when Ashley came over to her in the cafeteria that day at school. Amy was sitting at a table with Soraya when she walked up.

"Hi, Amy," Ashley said, crossing her arms and smirking. "I hear you're losing another boarder."

Amy glared at her.

"Oh, go away, Ashley," Soraya said.

Ashley ignored her. She was evidently on a mission. "You know," she commented, "some people might say it's a bit careless to lose two clients in one week. What *are* you doing to them?"

Amy's fingers clenched her fork as she felt her temper starting to rise.

"Just so you know, Mrs. Roche is delighted with the progress Swallow has made at Green Briar," Ashley said. "I rode him out on the roads yesterday, and he didn't even flinch. Of course, as my mom explained to Mrs. Roche, that's because *we* have the experience to deal with problem horses."

It was the last straw. Unable to bear the thought of Ashley riding Swallow, Amy jumped to her feet. "Experience!" she snapped, not caring that everyone around them was staring curiously at her and Ashley. "He was practically cured. You didn't have to do anything!"

Ashley had a ferocious smile on her face. "What a shame Mrs. Roche doesn't seem to agree with you." As she turned to go, she suddenly stopped. "Oh, by the way," she said. "Did you hear about my latest success? I took home two champion ribbons from the Meadowville show — First-year Green Hunter and Small Junior Hunter. It's a pity you don't have time to compete anymore. You used to be good." Smiling smugly, Ashley walked away.

That night when Amy got back to Heartland she found Lou talking on the phone. Her sister was frowning.

"No," she was saying, shaking her head. "No. We're not interested." There was a pause. "Yes, I appreciate that it *is* a good offer, Ted, but like I said, we're really not interested in selling." There was another pause. "Yes, of course I'll let you know if we change our mind. OK. Good-bye."

"Who was that?" Amy asked curiously as Lou put the phone down.

"Ted Grant," Lou replied. "He wanted to know whether we were interested in selling Heartland's land. Apparently they want to extend Green Briar." She must have seen the shock on Amy's face, because she added quickly, "I said no, of course."

"I can't believe that family!" Amy exclaimed, dumping her backpack on the floor. "Why can't they just leave us alone?"

"It was a very generous offer," Lou said.

"But we don't want to sell!" Amy said.

"Hey," Lou said, changing the subject. "We've had *some* good news today. I had an inquiry from a potential customer. A Mrs. Garcia. She's got a horse that won't load into a trailer. She's going to come by Saturday to have a look around."

"Great," Amy said.

Lou nodded, her blue eyes shining with relief. "I gave her a quote. She was very pleased — apparently it was fifty dollars less than Green Briar's."

Amy stared. "You gave her a quote?" Her voice rose. "But we don't give quotes!"

"Well, she asked for one," Lou said defensively.

"What else could I do? It normally only takes you about a week, doesn't it? I gave her a quote based on that."

Amy couldn't believe what she was hearing. "But we don't know what this horse is like. It might take a month!" she exclaimed. "You'll have to tell her that the quote can't stand. Tell her that we won't know until we've had the horse for at least a few days."

"I can't do that, it's not professional!" Lou objected. "We should have rates and stick to them. Everywhere else does."

"But we're not *like* everywhere else!" Amy cried, her frustration mounting. "That's the whole point of Heartland. Mom always treated each horse that came here as an individual."

"But, Amy —"

"No!" Amy said fiercely. "That's not changing, Lou. Not for anything!"

"OK, OK," Lou said, running a hand through her hair. "I'll guess I'll have to make it clear to Mrs. Garcia when she comes on Saturday."

Seeing the worry lines on Lou's face reappearing, Amy felt bad, but this was something she was determined never to give in about. It was one of the things that made Heartland so special — the belief that each horse was different and should be treated according to its needs. She wasn't about to let that change.

❧

On Saturday morning, Mrs. Garcia arrived. She was a tall, thin woman who looked immediately put out when Lou explained that the price she had been given was liable to change. "But you told me a price on the telephone," she said, standing in the kitchen.

Lou looked distinctly embarrassed. "I know. I'm sorry."

Amy tried to help her sister. "You see, we don't know how much it will cost until we've had the horse for a few days. All horses take a different amount of time."

"I see," Mrs. Garcia said coolly. She turned again to Lou. "So you're telling me that the price might change?"

"Yes, according to how long the process takes," Lou said. "But it might take only three days."

"Well, three days for an initial cure," Amy put in quickly, "but then another couple of days to make sure that the problem behavior has really gone."

Mrs. Garcia ignored her, obviously thinking of her as Lou's little sister and of no consequence. "Three or four days?" she said to Lou, sounding surprised. "At Green Briar they told me it would take at least ten."

Amy had seen her mom cure horses in even less — it was generally easy if you approached the problem with understanding and respect for the horse. However, she wanted to make things clear to Mrs. Garcia. Horses came to Heartland strictly on the understanding that Heartland decided on the type and length of treatment needed. "Sometimes, of course, they can take much longer — up to a month," she said, ignoring Lou's horrified stare, "or even six weeks."

"Six weeks!" Mrs. Garcia echoed, her eyes widening.

"Of course, I'm sure that wouldn't be the case with your horse, Mrs. Garcia," Lou said hastily.

"But you can't guarantee it," Mrs. Garcia said, stepping back, shaking her head. "No, I'm sorry. I think I'll take my horse elsewhere."

"But, really, Mrs. Garcia, like I said, it might take only three days," Lou said desperately.

But Mrs. Garcia was already walking out of the kitchen toward her car.

Lou turned on Amy. "Amy!" she said in frustration. "How *could* you? Now she'll go back to Green Briar, and we've still got an empty stable!"

"I only told her the truth," Amy said defensively.

Lou's eyes flashed. "The truth! You did your best to put her off."

"I did not!" Amy protested.

Lou shook her head. "Don't you understand? We're running out of money. If we don't get some paying clients soon, we're going to be in serious trouble. How are we going to feed the horses? How are we going to pay Ty? I can't write checks if we don't have any money in the bank." She took a deep breath. "Look, if we're going to survive, you may have to ease up on your principles for a bit."

Amy stared at her. "No!"

"Hi," a voice said tentatively. They both swung around. A tall, slim woman in her early twenties with blond hair falling to her shoulders in a mass of corkscrew curls was standing behind them, a worried frown creasing her forehead.

"Marnie!" Lou exclaimed.

Marnie looked from Amy to Lou. "Have I arrived at a bad time?"

"No," Lou exclaimed, hurrying forward. "Don't be silly! It's great to see you!"

"You, too," Marnie said, hugging her. "I parked in front and, er —" she raised her eyebrows quizzically, "heard the sound of voices in here."

Lou grinned. "I guess you couldn't exactly miss us." She turned quickly. "This is my sister, Amy."

Amy stepped forward. "Hello."

"Hi," Marnie said with a warm smile. "I've heard so much about you — and this place."

"Come on, we'll show you around," Lou said. She looked at Marnie's smart pantsuit. "Or do you want to get changed first?" she asked. "You might get a bit dirty."

"Who cares?" Marnie grinned. "Clothes can be cleaned. Come on. Show me the way."

Amy followed Lou and Marnie up the yard. She already had the feeling that she was going to like her sister's friend.

They met Ty in the back barn. "Good to meet you, Ty," Marnie said, shaking hands. Suddenly she caught sight of Sugarfoot, the tiny Shetland in one of the stalls, and gave a gasp of delight. "Isn't he the cutest thing!" The next second she was crouching down, saying hello to the little pony. The Shetland nuzzled her face, reveling as he always did in any attention. She looked up at Amy. "You're so lucky to live here. This place is great!"

Amy grinned at her, delighted by her enthusiasm.

"I always wanted to live somewhere like this when I was a kid," Marnie said as they walked around the rest of the yard.

"Where did you live?" Amy asked her curiously.

"New Jersey," Marnie replied. When they reached the front stable block, she looked into Pegasus's stall. "Hey, this fella doesn't look too happy," she said softly.

"He's not," Amy said, joining her at the door. There had been no improvement in Pegasus's condition. He was still not eating much.

"What's wrong with him?" Marnie asked curiously.

"We don't know," Lou said.

"He's had a blood test, but it didn't show anything,"

Amy said. Scott had called her the day after his visit to tell her that the results were inconclusive. "I think he's just missing Mom. He really loved her."

"Poor thing," Marnie said. "But he is going to get better?"

Get better? Amy felt her heart skip a beat as she looked at Marnie. Of course, Pegasus would get better. She hadn't even considered the possibility that he might not. "Yes — yes, he is," she said, nodding. She turned and looked at Pegasus. He had to. The thought of losing Pegasus was just too much to bear.

Amy and Lou helped Marnie unload her car, and then Lou showed her to their mom's old room. As she unpacked her two large suitcases, Marnie shook her head. "I've brought all these clothes," she said as she hauled one of the suitcases into the house, "but only one pair of jeans and a pair of shorts — I guess I'll be living in those."

"Don't worry," Lou said. "We can always find things for you to borrow."

Leaving Marnie to unpack and change, Amy and Lou went downstairs. A little while later, she joined them in the kitchen. "This is going to be so much fun," she said happily. She was dressed far more casually in a pair of cutoffs, a T-shirt, and sneakers, her wild hair tied back in a ponytail.

"I don't know about fun." Lou grinned. "There's lots of work to be done."

"Lou's got plans," Amy said warningly to Marnie.

Marnie raised her eyebrows. "Sounds scary."

"Oh, very," Lou teased her. She opened the fridge. "Do you want a cold drink?"

Soon they were all sitting around the table, drinking cans of soda. "So, come on," Marnie said to Lou. "Out with it, then. How about this change of lifestyle? It's so totally different from living in the rat race. How are you *really* coping?"

"Oh, you know," Lou said with a shrug. "I'm coping fine, though I guess I do miss some things."

"I should hope you do!" Marnie said. "All your friends miss you."

Amy felt a bit peculiar. She never really gave a thought to Lou's life in the city now. Lou seemed so much a part of Heartland that it was hard to remember that only three months ago she hadn't been to visit in more than two years and had lived her own separate life — with an apartment, boyfriend, and job — that Amy hadn't been a part of at all.

"And having the responsibility of things here is difficult," Lou continued. "I guess it's particularly bad right now, with Grandpa away."

"But there must be some positive aspects about living here," Marnie said.

Amy wondered what Lou would say.

"Oh, yes," Lou said. "There are lots of good things. I've rediscovered my love of horses and having a home like this and, well, just being here in the country is great."

Marnie grinned. "And what about the guys? Come on, what are *they* like around here?"

Lou blushed. "Oh, you know."

"I want more than that!" Marnie exclaimed. "Tell me all the gossip." She looked closely at Lou. "There must be someone or you wouldn't be turning that color." She turned to Amy. "Come on, Amy. You'll have to fill me in. Is there a new man in your sister's life since she dumped Carl?"

"I've been too busy, Marnie!" Lou protested.

"Amy?" Marnie questioned.

Lou jumped to her feet. "We should be helping Ty, not sitting around and gossiping."

"OK, then, you escape this time," Marnie said, getting up reluctantly. "But I'll find out," she warned as Lou headed for the door. "Just see if I don't."

🙟

In the afternoon, Amy went down to the field to bring Pegasus in. As usual, he was standing by the gate. She called his name, but his ears didn't even flicker. Her heart sank. He seemed to be getting worse instead of better with every day that passed. The remedies just didn't seem to be working. Patting his neck, she snapped the lead rope onto his halter. "Come on, then," she said softly. "Let's get you into your stable."

She clicked her tongue, but Pegasus didn't move. "Come on, boy."

With a deep sigh, Pegasus took a slow step forward and then another, the tips of his hooves dragging in the dirt. But then, suddenly, he stumbled, his feet slipping away beneath him. With a horrifying thud, his huge body crashed to the ground. He landed on his knees and fell almost immediately onto his side.

Amy felt as though the world had stopped. "Pegasus!" she gasped, throwing herself down beside him. He lifted his head.

Relief flooded through her. He was still alive.

"Pegasus! Come on! Up!" Amy urged, pulling his halter. "Come on, boy!"

The great horse looked at her. *No,* his eyes seemed to say, *I can't.* His head sank to the ground again.

Fear stabbed through Amy. She dropped the lead rope and raced up the drive.

"Lou!" she screamed. "Come quick!"

Chapter Five

Amy crouched by Pegasus's head, stroking him and talking to him softly. Marnie stood anxiously beside her. She and Lou had come running as soon as they heard her call.

Lou came hurrying down the drive toward them. "I called Scott," she said. "He's coming right away."

Amy looked frantically at her. "I can't find any bleeding, but he might have broken something. I can't tell with him lying down."

Lou took the lead rope. "Come on, Pegasus. Get up." But Pegasus didn't move. His eyes were half closed, his muzzle resting on the ground.

"Lou! What are we going to do?" Amy exclaimed, desperately wishing that Ty was there. But it was his half day, and he had left Heartland after lunch. "He might have broken something."

"Stay calm," Lou said, putting a hand on Amy's shoulder, utterly practical and efficient as always. "You won't help Pegasus by getting worked up."

"But I can't stay calm!" Amy burst out. Her breath was short in her throat, and her eyes filled with tears. "Pegasus! Please get up!" she pleaded.

"Look, I'll get some food," Lou said. "That might encourage him." She hurried off, returning a few minutes later with a bucket of pony cubes. She shook them, but Pegasus's eyes barely flickered in her direction.

"It's like he's frozen there," Marnie said, looking at Lou anxiously.

"It could just be shock after falling," Lou said. "Maybe he hasn't broken anything at all. Amy, what would Mom have used for shock?"

"Rescue remedy," Amy said.

"Can you go find some? I'll get a blanket. If he's in shock, it'll be important to keep him warm."

Through her panic, Amy saw the sense in Lou's words. Jumping to her feet, she raced to the medicine cabinet in the tack room. She pulled the dark brown bottle of rescue remedy from the shelf and ran back to Pegasus.

Crouching down beside him, she placed a few drops on the back of her hand and offered them to him. His nostrils flared slightly at the scent, and then he lifted his head and licked the drops off her hand. "Good boy," Amy murmured, delighted to see him move.

"What are you giving him?" Marnie asked.

"Bach Flower Rescue Remedy," Amy told her. "It's a mixture of different flower essences. Mom always used it for sudden trauma or shock."

Lou returned with a blanket and laid it over Pegasus's body. She glanced at her watch. "I wonder how long Scott will be?"

They watched Pegasus anxiously, each second dragging by. After five minutes, Amy was sure his eyes were looking clearer. He lifted his head slightly and his ears flickered. "The rescue remedy's working!" Amy cried to Marnie and Lou. She jumped to her feet and pulled on the lead rope. "Good boy! Come on, Pegasus! Up!"

With a huge groan of effort, Pegasus staggered to his feet. His head hung down, his knees were scraped and bleeding, and there was a gash on his right hock, but Amy was relieved that he didn't seem to have broken anything. She'd had a horrible image that when he stood up one of his legs would be dangling uselessly, but he was standing fairly evenly on all four legs.

Just as she started to check him over, there was the sound of a car tearing up the drive. Amy looked around. "It's Scott!" she said in relief, as the vet's battered Jeep pulled up outside the farmhouse. Throwing the door open, Scott jumped out and raced toward them.

❧

Half an hour later, Pegasus was back in his stall. It had been a slow process, but once there, Scott checked him over thoroughly, cleaned up his wounds, and gave him a shot of antibiotics to combat any infection. Amy watched from the door with Lou and Marnie. As Scott started to pack his equipment away, all the questions that she had been biting back while he treated Pegasus came surging to the surface.

"What's wrong? Why did he fall over?" Her voice rose. "Will he be OK, Scott?"

"He's weak because he hasn't eaten," Scott replied. "I think that's why he tripped and didn't get up. His injuries from the fall aren't serious." He frowned. "What really worries me is his lack of appetite."

"Do you have any idea why he's not eating?" Lou asked.

Scott looked serious. "It could be any one of a number of things." He looked at Amy. "Remember, he is an old horse."

"What do you mean?" Amy said quickly.

"Well, I'll have to do some tests. When I get the results, we'll have a better idea."

Amy couldn't speak. She felt hot tears well in her eyes.

"He'll be OK, won't he, Scott?" Lou said, her face pale.

There was an awful second of silence. "We'll have to wait and see," Scott said. He shook his head gravely, then looked at Amy. "He's getting older, and he's more prone to viruses now. What he's fighting is probably more serious than depression. I know this is hard to hear. You've got to consider the possibility —"

"No, I can't, Scott. I just can't," Amy sobbed. Pushing past Scott, she flung her arms around Pegasus's neck and started to cry as if her heart would break.

She heard Scott turn to Lou. "I think we just have to wait and see what happens over the next few weeks," he said. "We can see if anything shows up on the test results."

Amy sobbed loudly. What if Pegasus was really sick? How could she bear living without him? The straw rustled behind her and then she felt Lou's arm around her shoulders.

"It's OK, Amy," Lou said. "We can continue to treat him. Scott's not saying he won't get better."

"It's still too early to tell anything," Scott said slowly. "If the depression eases and he gets his spirit back, then he might be fine. We just have to keep an eye on him and see if he develops other symptoms."

Amy's heart lifted slightly. Maybe Pegasus would make a full recovery. She sniffed and looked up. "What can I do to help him?"

"Try anything you can think of," Scott told her. "You never know, something might work."

Amy nodded. "I'll try everything." She hugged Pegasus's neck. "I'll make you better, boy," she told him confidently. "I promise I will."

"Come on," Lou said softly, squeezing her shoulder. "We should let him rest."

❧

Back in the kitchen, Lou properly introduced Marnie and Scott.

"Nice to meet you." Marnie smiled at the vet.

"You, too," Scott said politely, and then seeing Lou trying to carry four cans over from the fridge, jumped to his feet. "Here," he said, "let me."

"Thanks," Lou replied, smiling.

As he took two of the cans from her, their hands brushed. Lou's cheeks flushed pink and Amy glanced at Marnie to see if she had noticed, but she had gone to the sink to wash her hands.

"So how's business?" Scott asked as Lou brought over some potato chips. "Any sign of things picking up?"

"None," Lou admitted.

"Well, I have some good news," Scott informed her. "I

think I might just have found you a new client, and not just any old client — Lisa Stillman."

"The one with the Arabians?" Amy said, feeling suddenly interested. There was a Lisa Stillman who owned a large Arabian farm about an hour away. Her horses were known throughout the state as superb show horses.

"That's the one," Scott replied. "I started treating her horses a few months back. Anyway, she's got a young mare who's recently become highly aggressive. She won't let anyone tack her up. I've checked her over and there's nothing physically wrong, so it has to be a behavioral problem of some sort. I suggested that she send her here."

"That's great!" Amy said. She turned to Lou in excitement. "Lisa Stillman's place is huge! If she likes us then we could get loads of work."

"The horse has been to two other stables already," Scott said, "including Green Briar. No one's been able to do a thing with her. Lisa's at her wit's end."

"Hey, Lou," Marnie said, "this could be your big break. Sounds like if you get in with this woman then you've got it made."

Lou's eyes lit up. "Is she going to phone us?" she asked Scott.

"Well, I said I'd talk to you and arrange a time for you to go over there so she can meet you," Scott replied.

"She's extremely particular about who she lets her horses go to. Most of them are very valuable animals." He scratched his head. "You know, I could give her a call and take you over there now, if you want. I've got to go anyway to see a horse I'm treating."

"That sounds great!" Lou said, but her face fell suddenly. "Oh, what about Pegasus? We shouldn't leave him."

"I'll stay," Amy said immediately.

Scott shook his head. "Lisa will want to talk to you about how you would go about treating Promise — her horse."

"Would you like me to stay with him?" Marnie offered.

"Thanks, Marnie," Lou said, "but it might be better if I stay. Pegasus will be happier with someone he knows."

Amy looked at Scott. She was sure she could see a hint of disappointment in his eyes, but he nodded understandingly. "Yes, I guess that would be best," he said. "Amy and I'll go."

"Can I tag along, too, then?" Marnie asked him. "I'd love to see this place."

"Sure," Scott said. "I'll call Lisa right now."

❧

Ten minutes later, Amy, Marnie, and Scott got into his car. Amy sat in the back, sharing the seat with Scott's big coat, a trunk of veterinary equipment, and a heavy flashlight. She pushed several map books and a box of medical supplies under the front seat so that she had room for her feet.

"Sorry it's such a mess back there," Scott said over his shoulder.

"I don't mind," Amy replied.

"So how long have you been a vet?" Marnie asked Scott as they drove off.

"Well, I got out of school six years ago," Scott replied. "And then I started specializing in equine work about three years ago."

Marnie smiled at him. "It must be a fascinating job." She twisted a strand of curly blond hair around in her fingers. "What do you like best about it?"

As Scott talked, Marnie nodded and smiled and laughed. It suddenly dawned on Amy that Marnie obviously hadn't realized that Lou liked Scott. Amy's eyes widened. She was flirting with him!

"So how long have you known Lou?" Scott asked Marnie.

"From when she moved to Manhattan," Marnie replied. "We worked for the same company. I —"

"I guess you know her ex-boyfriend then," Scott broke in.

"Carl?" Marnie said. "Yes. He's working in Chicago now."

"So, are they still in touch?" Scott's words sounded casual, but Amy picked up the slight edge to his voice.

"Not as far as I know. I think it's definitely over," Marnie said, looking a bit surprised.

"She hasn't spoken to him since they broke up," Amy put in. Lou and Carl's relationship had ended in a furious fight when Lou had discovered that Carl had set up a job for her in Chicago behind her back. It was a scheme to persuade her to move there with him.

Scott shook his head. "She's been going through a pretty tough time recently, hasn't she?" he said. "What with everything that's happened and deciding to give up her job and stay at Heartland. She's had to deal with some major life changes. But she seems to be coping really well."

Amy saw Marnie shoot him a sideways glance. Realization suddenly dawned on the older girl's face. "Yeah," she said, after a short pause. "Lou's great." Her hands dropped to her lap. "I couldn't ask for a better friend."

Lisa Stillman's farm was called Fairfield. It was set at the end of a long, straight drive bordered on each side by tall trees. Behind the trees, Amy could just catch tantalizing glimpses of Arabian horses grazing in lush fields.

They drove past an impressive white house and stopped. The barns were set up around a brick courtyard. Purple and pink flowers cascaded from large hanging baskets. Each dark wood stall door had a shining brass nameplate. Stable hands were bustling about, each wearing a green shirt with the Fairfield crest embroidered in purple on the pocket. It was the very picture of an old Virginia horse farm.

"Oh, wow!" Amy gasped, getting out of the car and spotting several beautiful Arabian horses looking out over the stall doors, their ears pricked and dished faces curious. "This place is amazing!"

Scott grinned. "I thought you'd be impressed." He shut his car door. "I'll go find out where Lisa is."

He walked over to speak to one of the stable hands. The second he was out of hearing range, Marnie turned to Amy. "You know what? I think he likes Lou!"

Amy nodded.

"You already knew!" Marnie groaned. She put her head in her hands. "And there I was, flirting like an idiot! But he's so cute!" She glanced up at Amy. "Lou likes him, doesn't she?" Marnie said, her voice hopeful.

"I'm pretty sure she does," Amy said.

"Oh, well, there goes my chance!" Marnie said with a laugh. "I guess that's life. So how come they haven't gotten together yet?" she asked curiously.

"I think it was a hard decision for Lou, breaking up with Carl," Amy replied. "And Lou and Scott have been getting to know each other slowly."

Marnie grinned. "Well, now that I'm here, we'll soon get things moving."

Scott headed back toward them, and Marnie stopped talking.

"Lisa's over in the office, apparently," Scott said. As they walked over to the redbrick building at the far end of the courtyard he said in a low voice, "She can be a bit odd — so be warned."

They walked into the office where a woman in her mid-forties was sitting behind a desk. She jumped up as soon as she saw them. "Scott!" she said, with an attractive, husky rasp to her voice. She had highlighted blond hair that fell onto her shoulders and a slim figure shown off by fitted cream breeches and an open-necked silk shirt. Amy stared. She didn't know what she had been expecting Lisa Stillman to look like, but certainly not anyone this glamorous!"

"How *are* you, darling?" Lisa said, coming around the desk, her arms outstretched. She kissed Scott on both cheeks.

"Fine." Scott turned quickly. "Let me introduce you. This is Amy Fleming from Heartland and a family friend, Marnie . . ." He paused.

"Gordon," Marnie said swiftly.

"Marnie Gordon," Scott repeated. "Amy's sister, Lou, had to stay with one of the horses — but I'm sure Amy will be able to answer all your questions."

Lisa looked at Amy. Her eyes were narrowed and skeptical. "How old are you?"

"Fifteen," Amy replied.

"Don't be put off," Scott said quickly. "Amy knows what she's doing, and Heartland has an excellent record."

Lisa turned to him. "Promise is a valuable horse. I'm not letting her go to a fifteen-year-old!"

"Lisa, Amy's got more experience than most people twice her age," Scott began.

"I have dealt with valuable horses before," Amy put in. There was a pause, and then Lisa looked at her. "I cured one of Nick Halliwell's best young horses of its fear of trailering recently," Amy said quickly, now that she had her attention. "And I am familiar with all the techniques my mom used at Heartland. She taught me everything she knew."

"And what sort of techniques are those?" Lisa demanded.

"Treating horses with kindness, respect, and understanding," Amy said, refusing to let herself be intimidated by this imposing woman. "Using rewards instead of punishments. Never bullying, never frightening." She put her chin up and met Lisa's eyes squarely. "Listening to the horse, mostly."

There was a moment's silence. Lisa raised her eyebrows thoughtfully and then suddenly, she nodded.

"OK," she said. "I like your attitude. You can treat Promise."

Amy felt an enormous rush of relief. For a moment she had been half expecting to be asked to leave.

"Come and see her," Lisa said.

Amy followed her out of the office, and Lisa pointed to a stall a few doors away. "That's her — the palomino."

An exceptionally pretty Arabian was looking over the stall door. A long creamy-white fringe fell over her face, her eyes were bright, her dark gray nostrils delicate and refined. Amy frowned. Everything about the mare's head suggested intelligence, softness, and sensitivity. "She doesn't look aggressive," she commented.

"She isn't," Lisa Stillman said, "until you try to ride her. Last week we got her tack on and took her in a show and she threw the rider and tried to bite the judge."

Amy walked forward slowly. Promise turned to look at her. Her ears pricked curiously, but Amy noticed that her eyes seemed reserved. Reaching the door, Amy stopped and gently stroked her. "What's her history?" she asked.

"I bought her six months ago from an elderly friend of mine," Lisa said. "She was selling her stock, and I was looking for a palomino. Promise had the perfect blood-lines and the perfect temperament — or so I thought," she added ruefully. "The first few days she was fine. But then one morning when a stable hand was saddling her up, he scolded her for fidgeting, and she turned and took a chunk out of his shoulder. When he smacked her she began kicking out. And things have gotten gradually worse since then. Whenever a saddle or bridle is brought close to her, she attacks anyone standing nearby, and if you try to mount, well, she bucks like crazy."

"But she was OK in her last home?" Amy said.

"Sure," Lisa said. "Half the time she was ridden by my friend's partially blind grandson. Apparently she never did anything wrong."

Amy looked at the palomino. She was standing, slightly aloof. "And she's been to other stables?" she asked. "What did they do with her?"

Lisa shrugged. "Tried to show her who's boss, I guess, but it didn't work. She's got some temper. And crops just seem to make her worse. The other stables sent her back in the end, telling me she's a rogue horse." She frowned. "But somehow I just don't believe it."

Looking at Promise's intelligent head, Amy didn't believe such words, either. Her mom had always insisted that rogue horses were virtually a myth. Yes, maybe there was the odd one who really couldn't be helped, but generally fear was at the root of all behavioral problems — and if that fear was dealt with, treated, and resolved, the attitude problems would go away, too.

"So, what do you think?" Lisa asked. "Can you help her?"

Amy nodded. Following her mom's reasoning meant that if she found the cause of Promise's fear, then stopping the aggression should be no problem at all. "Sure," she said honestly. "But I don't know how long it will take."

"You can have all the time you need," Lisa said firmly. "I just want her to be all right."

❧

"Hi, there!" Lou said, coming eagerly out of the house as Scott stopped the car. "How did it go?"

"Really well!" said Amy. "How's Pegasus?"

"No change," Lou said. "He ate a couple of carrots I offered him, but otherwise nothing to report."

"You should have seen this place, Lou," Marnie enthused. "It was amazing. Lisa Stillman has all these attractive stables set around a courtyard."

"And what about the horse?" Lou demanded.

"She's coming tomorrow!" Amy said.

"Really?" gasped Lou, her face lighting up. She turned to Scott. "That's wonderful!" For a moment Amy thought that Lou was going to throw her arms around his neck, but she seemed to control herself just in time. "Thank you so much for arranging it," she said to him.

"You've got Amy to thank," Scott said. "I just put the idea to Lisa; it was your sister who convinced her." He smiled. "But I'm glad that it's worked out," he said warmly. Their eyes met for a moment. Lou turned away, her face slightly pink.

Marnie nudged Amy and grinned.

After checking on Pegasus, Scott left. As soon as his car had disappeared around the first bend, Marnie couldn't contain herself any longer. She grabbed Lou's arm. "Lou!" she exclaimed. "That guy's crazy about you!"

Lou looked shocked. "What? Scott?"

"Yes! Who else?" Marnie grinned in delight. "Lou! He's gorgeous!" She shook her head. "I can't believe you didn't tell me about him!"

Lou didn't seem to know what to say. Her face turned crimson. "I — I didn't think there was anything to tell," she stammered.

"Hello, Lou!" Marnie exclaimed, throwing her hands up in the air. "This is *me* you're talking to. It couldn't be more obvious! All he did in the car was talk about you, didn't he, Amy?"

Amy nodded eagerly. "Yes, and he kept asking about Carl — if you were still seeing him."

"And, boy, did he seem pleased when we said that you weren't!" Marnie said. She grinned at Lou. "You're not going to tell me that you don't feel the same. I saw you just now, looking deep into his eyes." She mimicked Lou's voice. "'*Thank you, Scott. Oh, you're so wonderful, Scott!*'"

Lou burst out laughing. "I didn't do that!"

"Not much!" Marnie teased. *"Oh, Scott, I really don't know what we'd have done without you!"*

Lou buried her face in her hands. "OK! OK!" she cried. "So maybe I do like him." Her blue eyes shone as she looked at Amy and Marnie. "And you really think he might be interested in me?"

"Trust me," Marnie said. "I *know* he is."

Chapter Six

As soon as Amy woke up the next morning she hurried down to see Pegasus. He wasn't looking much better than the day before. "Good boy," she murmured, checking his cuts and scrapes. They had bled slightly in the night, so she got some hot water and carefully cleaned away the dried blood. Then she applied some comfrey ointment to help speed the healing process.

"Now let's get you something to eat," she said. "You have to build up your strength."

Seeing her walking up the yard toward the feed room, the other horses started to nicker hopefully. "In a minute," she told them. On this occasion, Pegasus had to have her undivided attention.

She chopped up three apples and, adding them to a small amount of bran and barley, mixed the food in a bucket with some beet juice and a spoonful of molasses. Then she hurried back to Pegasus's stall. He stared listlessly at the food and made no attempt to eat, so she took a handful and offered it to him. His lips grazed over her palm, taking up a bit of apple and some bran. "Good boy," she praised. She fed him a bit more and then a bit more. After twenty minutes he had just about finished the bucket. Feeling more hopeful, Amy patted him and then went to feed the other horses.

Just as she started filling the water buckets, Ty arrived. "Morning," he called, getting out of his car.

"What are you doing here?" Amy asked in surprise. It was Sunday, his day off.

"I thought you'd need a hand with the painting," he said, joining her at the tap. "I told Lou I'd come and help."

With everything that had happened the day before, it had slipped Amy's mind that today they were supposed to start painting and sprucing the place up.

"You forgot, didn't you?" Ty said, looking at her face.

"Kind of," she admitted. "But so much has been happening." She realized that Ty didn't know about the events of the day before. As the water buckets filled, she told him about Pegasus's fall and then about Lisa Stillman and Promise. It was a relief to be able to talk. That was the good thing about Ty, he always listened to her and understood.

When she had finished, Ty helped her take the water buckets to the stalls, and then they went to the house to talk to Lou about her plans. She and Marnie were in the kitchen, washing the breakfast dishes.

"So what do you want us to do?" Amy asked, opening the cookie jar and offering it to Ty before taking one herself.

"I thought if you two worked on the stalls and turning out the horses, then I could go pick up the paint and some brushes," Lou said.

"I'll help with the horses, too," Marnie offered.

Lou nodded. "When I get back we can paint the stable doors and then start cleaning out the tack and blanket rooms."

"If you get some wood, I could make storage trunks for the blankets, brushes, and extra tack," Ty said.

"Super," Lou said. "That will help things look better. Then I might get some new feed buckets and hay nets. They're not too expensive, and they'll look a lot better to new clients."

"How about some hanging baskets?" Marnie said. "Just two maybe, at each end of the front barn. You can put together really pretty ones, even with cheap plants."

Amy started to feel quite enthusiastic. She had thought that she didn't want any changes, but all these ideas would make Heartland look much better. "I'll call Soraya and Matt," she said. "I bet they'll come and help. We can give the yard a good sweep and straighten up all the pitch-forks and brooms. It's going to look great!"

❧

By lunchtime Heartland was a hive of activity. Amy and Soraya were busy painting the stall doors white while Lou and Matt freshened up the unpainted wood in the two barns with dark brown creosote. The tack room had been cleaned out and swept, and Ty was busy making large trunks to hold all the stuff that ended up in a pile on the tack room floor — polo wraps, bits, hoof picks. Marnie had filled two hanging baskets with red and yellow flowers and was sorting out the grooming kits, washing the brushes, and removing old caked hair from the currycombs.

Amy put a last brushful of paint on the stall door she was working on and then stood back to admire her work. "One more finished!"

"Everything is looking so much better," Soraya said, putting her brush down. She looked at Amy. "Which is more than can be said for you!"

Amy grinned. She had started off applying the paint carefully but had soon gotten bored and began to slap it on. Her jeans and T-shirt were covered with white splashes, and she was sure there must be some paint in her hair.

"It doesn't come off, you know," Soraya pointed out.

"Who cares?" Amy shrugged. "These jeans are old anyway."

Soraya shook her head and, picking up her brush, started to finish the last section of the door she was painting. "So, what was Fairfield like?" She was as crazy about horses as Amy and knew all about Lisa Stillman and her prizewinning Arabians.

"Very stylish," Amy said, and she told Soraya about the stable hands with their matching uniform shirts, the beautiful horses, and how glamorous Lisa Stillman was.

"Do you think she'll bring the horse here herself?" Soraya asked.

"She didn't say," Amy said. She wondered what Lisa would think of Heartland if she did come. Promise was supposed to arrive about four o'clock. She hoped they would have finished working on the yard by then.

"And this horse has a bad temper?" Soraya asked.

"Just when she's being ridden," Amy explained. "I think it's because something's frightened her in the past. She didn't look like a naturally aggressive horse." She saw that Soraya's door was just about done. "Should we start on the blanket room? There's a lot to go through in there."

By four o'clock the paint was almost dry, the blankets were sorted, and the tack had been put neatly away.

New trunks lined the back wall of the tack room, the bridles hung neatly on their correct pegs, and the halters were untangled, with their lead ropes tightly coiled. There were still a few things to do — the manure pile needed attention and the feed room still hadn't been swept or de-cobwebbed — but overall there was a huge improvement.

Amy stood drinking a soda with the others by the farmhouse and admired the bright white doors set against the dark wood, the hanging baskets filled with fresh flowers, and a yard that for once was almost free of hay and straw.

"Now we've just got to keep it like this," Lou said with a sigh of relief.

"Yeah, right, not with Amy around!" Matt joked.

Amy hit him. "Hey!"

There was the sound of a vehicle coming up the drive. They all turned to see a good-looking trailer with green-and-purple stripes heading toward them. "That must be Promise!" Amy said.

The trailer stopped just in front of them. The driver's door of the pickup opened and out jumped a tall, blond-haired boy. "Hey!" he said, looking a bit surprised to see such a crowd.

"Hi," Amy said. She felt slightly disappointed to see that the boy was alone. After all their work, she would have liked Lisa Stillman to see Heartland. She stepped forward. "I'm Amy."

The boy smiled. "Pleased to meet you, Amy," he said, holding out his hand. "I'm Ben Stillman. I'm delivering Promise for my aunt."

So that was why he looked a little familiar! Amy shook his hand and introduced everyone else. "We've been painting," she explained, suddenly realizing how messy she must look.

"I sort of figured," Ben said with a grin. He moved toward the trailer. "Should I unload Promise here?"

Amy nodded. "Yeah, that would be fine."

"Do you want a hand?" Ty offered.

"Thanks," Ben replied.

"He's cute!" Soraya whispered to Amy as Ben and Ty walked around the trailer to unbolt the ramp.

"I guess," Amy said, looking at Ben and feeling slightly surprised.

"Very cute!" Soraya said with a giggle as he disappeared into the trailer.

There was a clatter of hooves and Ben came out of the trailer, leading Promise. Amy caught her breath, all thoughts of Ben far from her mind. The mare pranced down the ramp with the grace of a ballet dancer. Her neck was arched, her golden coat gleamed, and her creamy white tail floated behind her. Reaching the ground, she stopped and snorted, wide nostrils flaring, soft dark eyes staring in surprise.

"She's gorgeous!" Amy breathed.

She glanced at Ty to see his reaction. He was nodding in agreement.

The mare whinnied loudly and then tossed her head and swung her hindquarters around. "Easy now," Ben said, patting her neck. He turned to Amy. "Where should I put her?"

"Over here," Amy said, leading the way to one of the empty stalls in the front block. Promise pranced in after him.

"High-spirited," Ty commented.

"Most Arabians are," Ben said, unclipping her lead rope. "She's OK — as long as you don't bring a saddle or bridle anywhere near her."

Promise looked over the stall door. Amy stroked her nose, admiring her sculpted face.

"I hope you can do something with her," Ben said. "You may be her last chance."

❧

After seeing Promise settle in, Ben left. Ty was going home and offered Soraya and Matt a ride.

"Thanks for all your help!" Amy called as they got into Ty's car. "See you tomorrow."

"Well, I could do with a long bath and a change of

clothes," Marnie said, looking down at her filthy jeans as they drove off.

"Me, too," Lou said. She looked at Amy. "But do you want a hand feeding the horses?"

"No, I'll be fine," Amy said. Ty had found time in the afternoon to make up the hay nets, so she just had to deal with the grain.

"I'll get dinner together, then," Lou said. "Coming, Marnie?"

They walked off into the house, and Amy made her way up the yard, enjoying the peace and quiet. It had been a hectic day. She stopped to check on Promise. The mare was standing at the back of her stall, pulling hay from the net. Hearing Amy's footsteps, she looked around.

"Hey, there, girl," Amy said, letting herself into the stall.

Promise looked at her for a moment and then continued to eat. Amy stood back, studying the mare. Her mom had always believed that a horse's personality could be read in its face. Amy looked at the mare's eyes. They were large, soft, and slightly triangular — thoughtful eyes, highly intelligent eyes. In fact, she thought, everything about Promise suggested intelligence. Her gaze wandered over Promise's delicate, fluted nostrils, shapely ears, and dished face with a slight moose nose. All of those features suggested that she was a horse that was alert, sensitive, proud.

A horse that would be fabulous to ride. One thing was for sure; she certainly did *not* look naturally aggressive.

It had to be fear that was causing her to act so out of character, Amy thought. When a horse was scared there were only three things it could do: flee, freeze, or fight. Looking at the pride and self-awareness mirrored in every line of Promise's beautiful head, it wasn't hard to believe that she had chosen to fight.

"Well, there's no need to fight me," Amy said, patting the mare's shoulder. "I won't hurt you or make you scared."

She left the stall feeling the first flicker of excitement that she always felt when facing the challenge of a new horse. She would make Promise ridable and show everyone that Heartland could run just as it always had, curing the horses that the rest of the world had given up on.

Suddenly feeling optimistic, she went to the feed room and began to fill the buckets. Maybe things were finally getting better, she thought as she added handfuls of soaked beet pulp to the grain. The yard was looking wonderful. If she cured Promise, then Lisa Stillman was bound to bring Heartland more customers. Best of all, she and Lou were getting along just fine. Yes, life at Heartland was looking up at last.

Amy started to pile the buckets up and then remembered Pegasus. Her newfound optimism faded slightly when she thought about the old gray horse.

She fed the other horses and then took Pegasus's bucket to his stall. He was standing quietly, his head low, his eyes depressed.

"Hey, boy," she said, looking over the door.

Hearing her voice, Pegasus lifted his head slightly. "I've brought you some supper," she said, letting herself into the stall.

Pegasus looked at the bucket, nudged his lips uninterestedly over the metal handle, and then dropped his head to the straw again.

"Come on. Eat," Amy urged, holding a handful of the feed by his nose.

With a sigh, Pegasus's lips moved over her hand, taking up some of the grain. Again, Amy fed him handful by slow handful. Pegasus ate listlessly, appearing to eat more to please her than out of any real sense of hunger. Amy consoled herself with the thought that at least he *was* eating something.

She kissed his forehead, willing him to recover, desperately searching in her mind for something more that she could do.

When he had finished the last handful of feed she began to massage his head and neck with T-touch circles. Pegasus rested his muzzle on his manger by the window and half closed his eyes.

"You like this, don't you?" Amy murmured. She swallowed as she remembered how Mom used to stand in the exact place, massaging Pegasus in the same way. Through the stall window she could see the evening shadows lengthening, and as she worked she thought of all the times when she had come out and watched Mom work her magic.

The minutes passed, her fingers moved over Pegasus's neck, and she felt herself relaxing. As the light in the stall began to fade it was as if the rest of the world had slipped away, leaving her and Pegasus alone — like it had once been just Mom and Pegasus. In the sweet-smelling stall, the past and the present seemed to merge into one.

Suddenly every muscle in Pegasus's body tensed. His head shot up and he stared out the window.

"What's the matter?" Amy said, following his gaze into the dusk.

She gasped, her heart standing still.

Amy didn't know if she could trust what her eyes were seeing. There, walking up the yard, hands in her barn jacket pockets, was a familiar figure. And the leap of Amy's heart made her believe that it really was her mom.

Chapter Seven

"Mom," Amy whispered, her insides felt numb as the figure walked toward her through the dusk. Then, without thinking, she flew to the stall door. *Could it be?*

Wrenching the bolt back with her trembling fingers, she stumbled out.

"Amy?"

Amy stopped in her tracks, feeling as if someone had just tipped a bucket of cold water over her. It was Marnie, hurrying toward her. Her hair was tied back, and she was wearing Marion's old barn jacket.

"Are you OK?" the older girl asked, looking at her shocked face in surprise. She followed Amy's gaze and looked down at the jacket. "Is it the jacket? Lou said I could borrow it."

Amy's mouth opened but she couldn't speak.

Marnie moved swiftly to her side. "I'll take it off if it upsets you. I'm really, really sorry."

"You looked so much like Mom." The words came out of Amy before she could stop them. She stared at Marnie, tears filling her eyes. For a moment, she had almost let herself believe. . . . She started to shake uncontrollably.

Marnie quickly put her arms around her. "Hey, it's OK," she soothed.

"In the dusk you looked just like her," Amy sobbed, overwhelmed by the rush of emotion. It was so real.

Just then there was a low whicker. Amy swung around. Pegasus had come to his stall door. His ears were pricked, and he was looking at Marnie. He tossed his head up and down.

"Pegasus?" Amy said, forgetting her own distress in her astonishment at seeing him look so alive. He pushed against the door.

"He doesn't think I'm your mom, does he?" Marnie asked.

Amy's eyes widened with sudden realization. "It's the jacket!" she exclaimed. "It must smell like Mom."

Pegasus whinnied again.

Marnie walked slowly up to his stall. Lowering his head, Pegasus rubbed against the jacket with his muzzle, breathing in and out in sharp, eager bursts. Marnie reached out and stroked his face. "I think you're right," she said to Amy. "He must remember."

"He looks almost happy again," Amy said, full of wonder. It was true. As Pegasus nuzzled the jacket, a kind of peace seemed to creep into his eyes. The tears dried on Amy's face. Suddenly she didn't care that Marnie was wearing her mom's jacket. Nothing mattered except the fact that Pegasus was looking like himself again.

Lying in bed that night, Amy found it difficult to get to sleep. She kept thinking of the moment when she thought it was her mother walking across the yard and of Pegasus's reaction. Her hopes rose. When she and Marnie had left his stall he was looking much happier. Maybe this was the breakthrough that she had been so desperately hoping for. Maybe now he would start to eat properly and get better.

She hurried out to feed the horses the next morning. However, even though Pegasus's eyes looked brighter, she found him as reluctant to eat as ever.

Her heart sank. "Come on, boy," she encouraged him, holding out a handful of feed. But instead of eating he simply nudged at the grain with his lips, spilling it into the straw.

In the end Amy had to give up. Time was passing, and

she had to get ready for school. But still she kept hoping. "Can you keep an eye on Pegasus today?" she asked Ty before she went to catch the bus. "I think he might start eating again."

"Sure," Ty nodded. "Have fun at school."

"Yeah, whatever," Amy replied, making a face. She threw her backpack onto her shoulder. "See you later."

As Amy walked along the corridor to her first class, she saw Ashley coming in the opposite direction. Amy tried to ignore her but Ashley stepped into her path, platinum hair falling glossily to her shoulders.

"So I hear you have one of Lisa Stillman's horses?" she demanded, crossing her arms. "Is it true?"

"Yeah," Amy replied, lifting her chin. "What's it to you?"

Ashley's green eyes were ablaze. "Lisa Stillman must have gone crazy. Why's she sending one of her horses to Heartland?"

"She's heard that we actually cure horses," Amy snapped, infuriated by Ashley's attitude. "Which is more than *you* apparently managed when Promise came to you."

Ashley's arched eyebrows rose. "So, it's that palomino?" Her perfectly made-up face suddenly creased into a smile. "OK," she said, nodding. "Now I get it."

"What do you mean?" Amy demanded.

"Well," Ashley replied. "It's not as if Lisa Stillman's letting you have one of her *valuable* horses. Everyone knows that palomino is a hopeless case. She's savage. Mom tried everything with her, but she never gave in, she just fought like crazy. What she needs is a bullet through her head."

"She does not!" Amy exclaimed furiously. "No horse deserves that."

"We'll see what happens to her when you can't cure her."

"I will cure her."

Ashley laughed mockingly. "In your dreams, Amy."

Feeling the anger inside her reaching boiling point, Amy pushed past Ashley.

"You'll never do it," Ashley called after her, her voice amused. "You haven't got the experience to cure any horse, let alone one like that."

Amy marched along the corridor, determined not to listen to Ashley any longer. Her words weren't true. She *was* going to cure Promise. She had never felt so determined about anything in her life.

As soon as Amy got home from school that afternoon she went to find Ty. He was cleaning the bridles in the tack room. "How's Pegasus been?" Amy asked.

"No change, really," Ty replied. He looked at her curiously. "What made you think he'd be different?"

Amy told him about what happened with the jacket the evening before. "I thought it might make him start eating again." She sighed. "But obviously not."

They were silent for a minute or two. "Are you going to work Promise this afternoon?" Ty asked.

Amy nodded. "I thought I'd join up with her first and then see how she reacts to the saddle and bridle," she said. Join up was a technique used to build a horse's trust. Marion had always used it as the first step in the rehabilitation of a horse, and she had taught it to Amy. "What do you think? I'm sure she's unmanageable just because she's scared. If I join up with her, hopefully she'll trust me enough to let me get the tack on."

"Sounds good. I can give you a hand, if you want," Ty offered.

"I'd like that," Amy said with a grateful smile.

Twenty minutes later she led Promise into the circular schooling ring at the top of the yard. The mare walked eagerly beside Amy, her steps short and fast, her eyes swiveling from side to side as she took in the unfamiliar surroundings.

Ty followed some distance behind with the saddle and bridle. Shutting the gate, Amy unclipped the longline from Promise's halter. Feeling herself free, the Arabian shied away, then cantered a few paces, and stopped dead a few yards from Amy. She sniffed at the sand.

With the longline coiled in her hand, Amy clicked her tongue and swept the lead toward the mare's hindquarters. Snorting wildly, Promise leaped into a high-headed canter. Amy moved quickly to the center of the ring and stood facing the mare. By pitching the longline toward the mare's rump, she urged her on at a canter. She knew that a horse's basic instinct was to see humans as predators and to try to escape if there was space to run. What Promise would learn through the join up was that Amy was a human who could understand her body language and be trusted.

After Promise had cantered around for several minutes, Amy stepped forward so that she was slightly in front of the horse. Immediately, Promise jerked to a halt and then swirled around and took off in the opposite direction. Amy's eyes were fixed on the mare's. Soon she saw the palomino's head starting to lower slightly and her muscles relax as her canter became smoother, the strides more rhythmical.

Still urging her on, Amy watched for the first signals of trust from the mare. After five or six circles the first one came. Promise's inside ear stopped moving; it seemed to stay fixed on Amy. It was a signal that the horse was getting tired and wanted to slow down. But for the moment

Amy kept her going, watching for the next sign. With most horses it took a while, but almost immediately Promise's head began to tilt so it was angled toward the center of the circle — closer to Amy. After a few more steps Promise lowered her head and neck, opening her mouth and looking as if she were chewing. It was her way of saying that she would like to stop, that she didn't want to run away from Amy anymore.

Quickly coiling in the line, Amy dropped her eyes from Promise's and turned her shoulders around. She stood and waited, trying not to tense up. She heard the soft thud of hooves on the sand behind her and the sound of the mare's breathing. She took a step and then paused. Suddenly she felt Promise's nose on her shoulder and warm breath on the back of her neck. It was join up!

Turning slowly and keeping her eyes lowered, because only predators stare, Amy rubbed the palomino between the eyes. Then, turning away, she walked across the ring. She listened closely. Would Promise follow her? If she didn't, then she would have to put her back to work and try again. But there was no need for a second try. After the slightest hesitation the mare followed her. Amy walked in a circle and changed direction several times with the mare following her every footstep. At last she stopped and rubbed Promise's head again.

"Good girl," she praised. The mare pushed her nose gently against Amy and then lifted her muzzle to Amy's face, snorting inquisitively. Amy smiled and rubbed her golden neck before turning to Ty, who was standing at the gate. "She was very quick to respond."

"She's very smart," Ty said. "She knew what to do right away."

"That's what I thought!" Amy said.

They exchanged smiles. Amy felt a warm glow of happiness spread through her.

Turning back to Promise, she started on the next stage of her plan. She ran her hands over the mare's neck, withers, back, hips, and flanks, all the vulnerable areas that a horse would be uneasy about letting a predator near. Promise stood rock solid.

Feeling confident, Amy snapped the longline onto Promise's halter and called to Ty to bring the tack into the ring. Now that Promise trusted her, she was sure that the mare would let her put the saddle and bridle on her.

But as Amy stepped forward to take the saddle from Ty, Promise suddenly exploded. Pulling back, she reared up on her hind legs, her front hooves lashing angrily through the air. Amy leaped back just in time. Dropping the saddle on the ground, she moved quickly to the mare's shoulder, closing in on her head as soon as her hooves touched the ground. "Easy now," she said. "Easy." For a moment Promise's eyes seemed to flash and she fought Amy's hold on her halter, but then she settled.

Glancing around, Amy was relieved to see that Ty had acted quickly and whisked the saddle away. Balancing it over the gate, he now headed back toward her. "That was close!" he said breathlessly.

Amy nodded, feeling confused. She was certain that the join up had gone well and that Promise wasn't afraid of her, so why did she react so violently to the saddle?

"I'll send her around again," she said, unclipping the longline.

Ty moved to the side, and Amy sent Promise around the ring once more. The join up went even quicker this time. Within two circuits Promise was licking her lips and lowering her head, asking permission to stop. As soon as Amy coiled the longline and turned around, Promise joined her and followed her trustingly around the ring.

Ty brought the saddle over. But almost immediately, Promise was on her back legs, rearing and striking out. Ty hastily backed off.

"I can't understand it," Amy said when Promise was standing still beside her again.

"Maybe it's something else," Ty said, joining her without the saddle this time. Promise bent her head toward him. "Maybe the saddle hurts her."

Amy shook her head. "Scott said that he's checked her over thoroughly and there's nothing wrong. It has to be fear." She frowned. "So what do we do now?"

"We could leave an old saddle in her stall," Ty suggested. "That way she'll see it all the time and get used to it."

"Good idea," Amy said, nodding quickly. "If we leave it there overnight, then we can try again tomorrow."

"Let's put some powdered valerian in her feed," Ty said. "That should help her relax."

Amy started to lead Promise toward the gate. "It's funny," she said, looking at the mare's intelligent head. "She doesn't look like the fearful type, and she seems confident about everything else."

"Fear's like that, though," Ty commented. "Horses can be afraid of some crazy things, just like people."

Amy nodded. She guessed he was right, and yet something about the way the mare had reared bothered her. She went over the moment in her mind. As the mare had struck out, Amy had caught a glimpse of her eyes and they hadn't looked scared.

Amy pushed the thought away. Of course it was fear — fear was at the root of nearly all behavior problems. That's what Mom had always said. She had also said that you shouldn't rush a horse. Amy knew they just had to be patient. They would work Promise slowly, and eventually she would get over her fear.

❧

Before going into the house for the night, Amy put an old saddle in the palomino's stall. As she walked in with the saddle over her arm, Promise shied away, flattening her ears and throwing her head in the air.

"It's OK," Amy said, dropping the saddle to the floor. "I'm not going to put it on you." She waited outside to see how long it would take Promise to leave the back of her stall.

To her surprise, before she had even bolted the door, Promise walked over to the saddle and began sniffing it curiously. Then with apparent disinterest, Promise turned to her hay net and continued to munch her hay. She didn't seem bothered by the saddle at all.

Strange, Amy thought. Usually a horse took quite a while to get used to an object that scared it. Apart from when Amy had been carrying the saddle, Promise had shown no hint of fear or unease. She guessed the valerian might have kicked in. But to have such a change, so soon? It wasn't normal. Not knowing what to think, Amy went into the farmhouse.

Lou and Marnie were sitting at the kitchen table, talking and poring over a page of figures. Their faces were serious.

"Hi!" Amy said.

"Hi," Lou replied.

Marnie smiled quickly at Amy and then turned back to the papers and continued the conversation. "There has to be something we can do."

"What are you talking about?" Amy said, looking over their shoulders.

Lou shuffled the papers together. "Nothing."

Amy looked from one to the other. "What's going on?"

Marnie sighed. "You should tell her, Lou."

"It's OK," Lou said quickly to Amy. "Just some financial worries."

"Oh," Amy said, feeling slightly relieved that it wasn't anything serious. They always had money problems. She opened the cookie jar and took out a couple of cookies. She turned and found Lou looking at her.

"You're not concerned, are you?" Lou said slowly.

Amy shrugged. "We always have money problems. We'll manage. We always do."

"Amy, we've got to face the facts!" Frustration showed clearly on Lou's face. "We really need to get some more clients."

"We've got Promise," Amy retorted.

"One horse?" Lou shook her head. "Amy, we can't run this place on the fees from one horse!"

"So what are you saying?" Amy demanded. "We just give up?"

Lou's response was swift. "No, but we have to think of something. And fast." Lou put her head in her hands. "I didn't want to tell you," she said hopelessly. "I know how worried you've been about Pegasus and how pleased you were to get Promise but, yes — unless we get some new clients very soon, we could have a real problem."

"It's really that bad?" Amy asked.

There was a horrible silence.

Marnie looked at her. "Lou and I have been trying to think of something, looking over the figures, looking at the assets. But she's right, Amy. It's not a good situation."

Amy took a step back, horrified. "But it can't be. What about the brochure and the advertising?"

"They haven't brought us any new business yet." Lou stood up. "Amy, we can't pretend any longer. If things don't get better fast, we'll have to close the place down."

Chapter Eight

Amy hardly slept that night. She tossed and turned, thinking over and over what Lou had said. Heartland couldn't close. There had to be something they could do to keep it open. At five thirty she gave up trying to sleep and, pulling on her jeans, went outside.

The early light was pale, and the only sounds were the birds singing in the trees. Feeling sick with worry, Amy carried a saddle up to the circular training ring and then got Promise's halter. The only plan that she had been able to come up with was to cure Promise as quickly as possible in the hope that Lisa Stillman would send them more horses.

Amy led the palomino up to the ring and went through the process of joining up again. As the sun rose and the light brightened, Amy tried putting a saddle on the palomino's back, but as soon as she had lifted the saddle off the gate the mare reared and fought. Eventually Amy gave up and took Promise back to her stall.

Before returning the halter to the tack room, Amy looked over Pegasus's door. He was lying down, his muzzle resting on the straw, his breathing labored. "Pegasus?" Amy said in alarm.

Pegasus staggered to his feet. His ribs were sticking out, and the hollows in his sides moved in and out as he breathed. Amy went into his stall and checked him over. His breathing seemed to steady a bit. But he still didn't look well. Putting an arm over his back, Amy laid her face against the swell of his shoulders and felt tears well in her eyes. What else could she do?

"Amy?"

She jumped and swung around. Ty had arrived and was leaning on the half door. "You OK?" he asked in concern.

"Yeah," she said quickly, brushing her eyes with her hand. "I'm fine." But as she met Ty's concerned look a sob leaped into her throat. "I don't know what to do, Ty," she burst out helplessly. "I've tried everything. Nothing's working." She looked at him desperately. "What else can I do? There must be *something*!" Amy said in frustration. "*Mom* would have thought of something!"

She saw a muscle in Ty's jaw tighten.

"If only she were here!" Amy murmured, looking down to the ground.

"If only," Ty said quietly. With a sigh, he straightened his shoulders. "Look, you stay here. I'll go start the feeds."

Amy watched him leave and, burying her face in Pegasus's mane, she tried to fight back her tears.

As Amy walked down the drive to catch the school bus, a turmoil of thoughts ran through her head — Pegasus, Promise, Heartland's future. Then as she passed Pegasus's empty paddock she felt overwhelmed with sickness.

On the bus, she hardly said a word. Soraya and Matt seemed to sense that she didn't want to talk and left her alone. Several times she caught them exchanging worried looks.

"I'll see you guys later," Matt said quickly as they got off the bus. "I . . . I need to check the roster for tonight's game." Shooting a look at Soraya, he hurried away.

"So what's up?" Soraya asked as she and Amy walked to their lockers.

Amy didn't answer. She didn't know what to say or where to start.

"Is it Pegasus?" Soraya asked.

"Yes. Well, partly," Amy said. She hugged her backpack to her chest. "He's worse."

"Oh, Amy, I'm really sorry," Soraya said, her eyes filling with sympathy.

"Nothing I do seems to make a difference," Amy said. "I just can't seem to cure him."

"I'm not surprised," Ashley's voice drawled.

Amy swung around. Ashley was standing behind her with Jade.

"So the healing hands aren't working?" Ashley prodded, her green eyes dancing at Amy's discomfort. Jade smirked. "A healer who can't even heal her own horse. That's just too bad."

"Give it a break, Ashley," Soraya snapped with unusual force. She put her hand on Amy's arm. "Come on, Amy, let's go."

Feeling too drained to cope with Ashley's taunts, Amy turned away.

"When are you going to face it, Amy?" Ashley called after her. "You and your sister are never going to make Heartland work without your mom."

Amy stiffened, but just as she was about to retaliate she was struck by the painful realization that Ashley's words might be true.

"Come *on*," Soraya hissed, pulling her arm.

Amy followed Soraya dumbly. For the first time in her life, she was doubting herself and her own abilities.

Maybe I'm not good enough to save Heartland, she thought. *After all, Promise won't let me near her with a saddle, and Pegasus is getting worse.* She started to feel sick again. She wouldn't let Ashley be right.

By the time Amy got home from school and started the long walk up the drive, she was feeling intensely depressed. Instead of the leap that her heart normally made on coming home again, she felt it sink at the thought of all the problems awaiting her.

To her surprise, as she reached the house the back door flew open. "Amy!" Lou said, her eyes shining. "We've been waiting for you to get home! Marnie and I have had an idea!"

"An idea," Amy echoed, following her into the kitchen.

Marnie was standing by the sink. "A way of getting new customers for Heartland," she said, excitement lighting up her face.

Amy's hopes leaped. "What is it?"

"We can organize an open-house day," Lou declared. "But not just for people to come and look around; one where we actually *show* people what we do. You could demonstrate joining up with a horse, and Ty could explain the treatments we use, you know, the aromatherapy and the herbs and the . . ."

"I don't think it will work," Amy responded.

Lou stared at her. "Why not? It would definitely get us customers. Most of them have never seen a join-up demonstration before — it's a magical experience!"

Amy shook her head desperately. After Ashley's words that afternoon the last thing she wanted was people coming out to Heartland. What would she say if they asked her about Promise? What would they think when they saw Pegasus? Ashley's words echoed in her head — who would want to send a horse to Heartland when she couldn't even cure her own horse?

"But, Amy," Lou said, looking at her in surprise. "Don't you see? This could be the answer to our problems."

"Lou's right, Amy," Marnie said. "I'm sure that if people actually see how you work they will be really interested in sending problem horses here."

"I can't do it," Amy said firmly.

"But . . ." Lou began.

"Lou, I just can't. Please don't make me, not now," Amy said in almost a pleading tone.

Lou's temper suddenly seemed to snap. "Oh, for goodness' sake, Amy! What's the matter?" she shouted angrily. "Don't you realize that this is our last chance? You can't just say no!"

"But, Lou," Amy shouted back, "you don't understand. There's just too much going on. Everything's going wrong!" Flinging her backpack down, she ran out of the house.

She headed for the stable block, overwhelmed with emotion. It felt like her world was collapsing. Seeking comfort, she went into Pegasus's stall and threw her arms around his neck. "Oh, Pegasus, what are we going to do?" Burying her face in his mane, she breathed in his sweet smell and wished that everything could be different.

A few minutes later there was a faint knock behind her. "Amy?"

She turned. Marnie was standing in the doorway.

Pegasus whickered softly. Ever since the evening when Marnie had been wearing the jacket, he seemed to have taken a liking to her. He stretched out his nose. "Hi, big fella," Marnie said, stroking him.

Amy swallowed her tears.

"Um . . ." Marnie said hesitantly. "Lou's a little upset, Amy."

Amy didn't say anything.

"The open house is a really good idea," Marnie said. "Why don't you want to do it?"

Amy looked at Pegasus. His ribs were poking out, his white coat looked stark and dull. "How can we have people here?" she said hopelessly. "When I can't even cure Pegasus, my own horse?" A lump of tears swelled painfully in her throat. "It's no good," she said, shaking her head. "I'm no good."

Marnie looked at her in genuine astonishment. "But that's crazy. Lou's told me about all the horses you've cured — little Sugarfoot, and Nick Halliwell's horse, and the horse that was in the accident."

"But I'm not Mom," Amy whispered, hot tears in her eyes. "She would have cured Pegasus. She would have known what to do with Promise."

Marnie's blue eyes searched Amy's face. "But your mom had years and years of experience. Do you think she got it right all the time when she was first starting? She would have made mistakes, had failures. But she didn't let that stop her." She took Amy by the shoulder. "Anyway, for all you know, the vet said Pegasus could have a sickness you can't cure — something that even your mom wouldn't have been able to cure."

Amy bit her lip.

"Amy," Marnie said softly. "Stop being so hard on yourself. You can't be Marion. All you can do is be yourself and listen to your own instincts."

There was a deep moment of silence. "Mom used to say that," Amy whispered. "She always used to say that I had to trust my instincts."

"So *do* it!" Marnie said. "Look, Heartland can be a success, I'm sure of it. But only if you run it in your own way and for your own reasons, and only if you and Lou work together as a team. You are both very talented, in different ways. You're great with the horses, and Lou knows what she's doing with the books and business side of things. You have to find a way to use those talents together to really help Heartland."

Slowly, Amy nodded and then took a deep breath. "I'll — I'll think about the open house."

Marnie smiled. "Good. I really think it could work." She hugged Amy. "And remember what your mom said — trust your instincts."

Amy watched her leave the stall. *Trust my instincts.*

As she stroked Pegasus's neck the truth hit her. She had been so busy thinking about what Mom would have done that she had forgotten to listen to her own instincts. Not only that. She had also forgotten her mother's absolute rule — *listen to the horse.*

That evening when the last of the work had been done and Ty had left, Amy led Promise to the schooling ring. Following the pattern of her previous sessions with the horse, she joined up with her and then picked up the saddle from the gate. However, this time as Promise backed up defensively, Amy watched her eyes.

It was hard to believe, but Amy was certain that she saw no fear.

Dropping the saddle, Amy quickly moved Promise

away, talking to her and leading her around until she was calm again. Then she stopped and thought.

At the sight of the saddle coming near her, Promise's eyes had filled with anger and — Amy struggled to find the right word. *Resentment.* Yes, Promise had looked resentful.

For a moment, Amy looked at the horse. *Why?* She thought about everything she had heard about Promise. As she remembered the details of Promise's life prior to belonging to Lisa Stillman, Amy suddenly had a feeling that she was close to finding what was at the root of the problem.

Unclipping the longline, she set Promise loose in the empty field next to the training ring and secured the gate before hurrying across the yard to the house. To her relief, there was no one in the kitchen. She picked up the phone.

A quick call to Scott gave her the telephone number that she wanted. She punched the numbers and waited, still not totally sure what it was that she was trying to find out.

When the phone was picked up, an older woman answered. "Eliza Chittick speaking," she said briskly.

"Hi," Amy said. "This is Amy Fleming from Heartland Sanctuary. I have a horse you once owned — Promise, a palomino. I'm working with her for Lisa Stillman, and I was wondering if you could help me with some details about her background."

"Promise?" Mrs. Chittick said, her voice immediately softening. "Why, sure, I can help. Fire away."

Amy explained about Promise's reaction to the saddle and bridle.

"I'd heard from Lisa she was being difficult," Mrs. Chittick said, sounding worried. "But I had no idea it was this bad. She was perfect when she was here. A horse in a million. Did Lisa tell you that my grandson used to ride her? He's almost blind, and she's the only horse I would have trusted with him."

"Yes, she told me about that," Amy said, still not quite sure what information she was hoping to get from Mrs. Chittick but feeling sure that the key to Promise's behavior was somehow connected to her past. "So she was good with him?"

"Wonderful," Mrs. Chittick said. "We trusted her completely, and she seemed to understand that she needed to take special care of him. He'd ride her bareback with just a halter. I've never known a more intelligent horse. She acted more like a human than a horse, really." Amy heard her smile. "And I guess that's how we treated her. Somehow, when you were doing things with her, you almost felt that you had to ask her permission."

Something in Amy's brain suddenly seemed to click

into place. *That was it!* Her fingers gripped the receiver in excitement. She was sure that she had figured it out.

"Like I said, she was a horse in a million," Mrs. Chittick continued. "I just can't believe that Lisa's having these problems with her. The horses are treated well at Fairfield. I can't understand what's gone wrong."

Amy thanked Mrs. Chittick for the information and promised to call her with news about Promise's progress. Putting the receiver down, she leaned against the wall. Yes, at Fairfield the horses were undoubtedly treated well — but they were treated like horses. And that wasn't what Promise had been used to.

Amy hurried back to the field. Promise was grazing in the fading light, but as Amy undid the gate, she walked over, her head outstretched, her delicate ears pricked. Amy rubbed her forehead and tried to imagine what it must have been like for Promise. All her life she had been treated as an individual, trusted, respected — *loved* — and then suddenly she had been uprooted from everything she knew and placed in a yard where she was treated like any other horse.

Amy remembered what Lisa Stillman had said about the first day that Promise had been tacked up. Amy could picture how it happened when the tack was thrown swiftly onto Promise's back — she tried to object to what she felt was rough handling but she was slapped by the stable hand. Then Promise retaliated by biting and was punished further.

Amy studied Promise's head — confident, intelligent, bold. Whereas most horses would have submitted to the discipline, Promise had chosen to fight the firm handling with aggression. It was her way of saying that she wanted to be treated better, but the stronger people got with her, the more aggressive she had become. Arabians were a proud breed, and every line of Promise's body, every contour of her head suggested that she had an extreme sense of pride. She was a horse that would never give in to harsh treatment.

"But I wasn't strong with you," Amy whispered to the golden horse. "So why fight me?"

Think like the horse, she thought to herself. She looked at the saddle and imagined it from Promise's point of view. After the first time when she kicked at the stable hand, the staff at Fairfield would have approached saddling her with firm words and ready slaps. And each time Promise would react aggressively. Maybe now the sight of someone carrying a saddle was enough to make Promise go wild. Even though joining up was powerful, it had not been enough to show Promise that she was respected and trusted. Somehow Amy had to break Promise's negative feelings. She needed to show Promise that the sight of the saddle didn't mean she'd be mistreated.

So what do I do? Amy thought.

She stood for a moment, looking at the horse, and then, all of a sudden, she knew. She clipped the longline onto Promise's halter and stroked the mare's neck. Then she moved her hands and pressed experimentally on the mare's back.

Promise turned and looked at her.

"May I?" Amy whispered.

Promise turned her head back to the front. Taking a deep breath, Amy took hold of the long, creamy mane and vaulted onto Promise's back. As she landed she tensed, half expecting her theory to be wrong and the mare to explode with a defiant rear, but nothing happened. Promise stood still and steady.

Amy relaxed. "Walk on," she said, squeezing with her legs. Promise moved forward, her body warm under Amy's legs.

Amy guided her around the field, using the halter and pressure from her knees. Promise seemed calm and happy, striding out, her action smooth and effortless, her ears pricked. After a few circuits Amy gave her a pat and asked the mare to trot. Her stride was bouncy, but Amy relaxed into it, letting her body absorb the bounces.

She stroked Promise's neck. After a few moments she couldn't resist it any longer — leaning forward she urged the mare into a canter. Promise leaped forward, her ears pricked. Amy grasped the mane, her body forward, her eyes alight. She could feel the energy surging through Promise's muscles, feel her quarters gather and push.

"Faster," she whispered.

With a surge, Promise's stride lengthened. Her mane whipped back into Amy's face, the wind dragging tears from Amy's eyes. Bending low over her neck, Amy lost herself in the thunder of hooves and the power and speed of the golden horse beneath her.

At long last, she slowed Promise down, eased her to a trot, a walk, and finally to a halt. Leaning forward, she kissed Promise's neck and then slid off. Promise nuzzled Amy's shoulder and then, lifting her muzzle to Amy's face, blew in and out. For the first time since she had come to Heartland, her eyes looked genuinely happy.

"Now let's see about the saddle," Amy said. She hitched Promise to the fence and got the saddle from the schooling ring. Walking back through the gate, she watched Promise's reaction carefully. Promise turned and looked but did nothing else. Amy could feel her heart speeding up in her chest. She approached the horse. She reached Promise's side.

"May I?" Amy asked, offering the saddle to the mare. Promise snorted but did not move.

Holding her breath, Amy lifted it up and gently slid it onto the mare's back.

Promise stayed still.

Fingers trembling, Amy did up the girth. The saddle was on. She pulled down the stirrups and, not bothering with a bridle, mounted Promise.

Nothing happened.

Amy stroked Promise's neck in delight. "Walk on."

After several times around the field, Amy halted Promise by the gate. Dusk had fallen, but Amy was so elated that she hardly noticed. Promise had let Amy saddle and ride her! She knew that it wasn't enough for Promise to trust just one person to tack her up, but that could be worked on. Amy dismounted and hugged the mare.

The breakthrough had been made.

Chapter Nine

The following morning, Amy woke early again and hurried out of the house. If she was quick she would have time to work Promise before school. She hadn't told Lou and Marnie about the previous night's success. It had all felt somehow unreal, and she decided to ride Promise one more time before she told anyone.

The palomino was looking out over her stall door. She whinnied softly when she saw Amy, her eyes shining. Amy felt a warm glow of happiness. Suddenly she just knew that Promise was going to be OK, and she knew she wanted to help Lou with the open house. Amy wanted to do whatever she could to save Heartland and help more horses like Promise.

She got the mare's halter, but before returning went to check over Pegasus's door.

Her heart stopped.

Pegasus was lying on his side, his head and neck stretched out in the straw. For an awful moment Amy thought he was dead, but then she saw his side rise and fall.

Dropping the halter she fumbled with the bolt and ran into his stall. "Pegasus?" she gasped.

The great horse lifted his head slightly. His nostrils quivered in a faint whicker, and then his head fell to the straw again.

An icy feeling closed in on Amy's heart. She stood undecided for a moment and then turned and raced to the house. "Lou!" she screamed, flinging the door open. "Lou! Quick!"

A few seconds later, Lou came stumbling into the kitchen, her eyes blinking, her hair uncombed. "Amy, what's the matter? It's only six o'clock."

"It's Pegasus!" The words left Amy in gasps. "He's down in his stall. I don't think he's going to get up again."

The sleepiness left Lou's face in an instant. "I'll call Scott. You go back to Pegasus. I'll be out as soon as I'm dressed."

Amy ran back to Pegasus's stall. He was lying there, motionless. Amy knelt by his head. His eyelids flickered, and lifting his head slightly, he rested his muzzle against her knees. He groaned quietly. Bending over, Amy cradled his huge head in her arms, kissing his ears, his eyelids, the soft skin above his nostrils. Her fingers rubbed his head and neck frantically. "It's OK, boy," she said. "It's going to be OK." She repeated the words over and over again, desperate to believe them, to somehow make them true. But deep down she knew the awful truth. It was the end — Pegasus was dying.

There was the sound of running footsteps. Marnie appeared in the stall doorway. "Lou's talking to Scott now."

At the sound of her voice, Pegasus lifted his head, and for one brief second his eyes seemed to brighten. But then he sighed and his head sank to the ground again.

"Is there anything I can get you?" Marnie said to Amy.

Amy shook her head, tears blurring her eyes. "I don't think so." Looking at Pegasus's side, she saw that his breathing was getting shallower. She stroked his cheek. His half-closed eyes were dull. It was as if the spark inside him that had started to fade when Marion died had finally gone out. Amy suddenly looked at Marnie. "The jacket!" she said.

Marnie's eyes widened with realization. "You mean your mom's barn jacket?"

"Yes," Amy said quickly. "Where is it?"

"In my room."

"Can you get it, please?" Amy whispered. "I think it might help."

Marnie hurried back to the house.

Amy stroked Pegasus's head. "There, boy, it's going to be just fine. You'll see."

Lou arrived at the stall. "Scott's on his way," she said. She knelt down beside Pegasus. "Hey, boy," she said softly.

Just then, Marnie came back with the jacket. "What do you want me to do with it?"

"Hand it to me," Amy said. As she reached for it, Pegasus caught its scent. Lifting his head, he whinnied hoarsely and, making a great effort, reached toward the jacket. All three of them said nothing, their eyes fixed on his face.

Pegasus breathed in and then out for a long moment. Then, seeing his head about to fall, Amy folded the jacket onto her knee and Pegasus lowered his head so it rested gently in her lap. Blinking back the tears, Amy stroked his face as he nuzzled the worn fabric. He looked more at ease, but his breathing was growing more shallow. And then his eyes closed and he sighed.

Amy started to sob. "Oh, Pegasus, please don't die! *Please!*"

Lou put an arm around her shoulders. "His body is old," she said softly. "He's lived a long, full life."

Just then there was the sound of footsteps coming up to the stall. Amy glanced around. It was Scott. One look at his face was enough.

"Scott, there has to be something we can do," Amy sobbed.

Scott shook his head sadly as he looked at the horse. "Amy, you've given him a wonderful home, an ideal life. But life doesn't last forever."

"But Mom, Mom would want us to try," Amy cried in anguish.

"Your mom would understand, Amy," Scott said as he crouched down beside her and ran his hand over Pegasus's shoulder and chest. "I didn't want to worry you, but you see these swellings?" he said, pointing out a number of small fluid-filled lumps on the underside of Pegasus's chest. Amy nodded. "They suggest he has a kind of internal tumor, a lymphosarcoma, I'd guess," Scott told her.

"A tumor . . . *cancer*?" Amy stammered.

Scott nodded. "I suspected it last time I saw him." His eyes sought hers. "And the last batch of tests came back late last night. They were positive. Amy, there isn't anything we can do to cure him. Some diseases simply can't be healed." He paused. "We can't let him suffer, Amy," he said solemnly. "It wouldn't be fair."

Amy bit hard on her lower lip, desperately struggling to hold back the sobs that were threatening to shake her body. Part of her wanted to cling to every last moment she had with Pegasus. But Scott was right, she couldn't let him go through this any longer. However painful it would be, she had to do what was best for the horse she loved.

"Amy?" Scott said softly.

Amy looked up at him. She knew he was asking permission to put down her beloved Pegasus. Everything was blurred. All she could see was Pegasus's head in her lap, his eyes flickering. With tears streaming down her face, she nodded.

"It won't take long," Scott said, opening his black bag and taking out a needle. "He won't feel a thing. I promise. You're doing what is best for him."

For the last time, Amy bent her head to Pegasus's. His eyelids blinked. "I love you, Pegasus. I always will," she whispered, hot tears falling on his face. "Good-bye, boy."

She kissed his muzzle, and then looked to Scott, her eyes foggy with tears. She cradled Pegasus's head as Scott administered the injection.

A few long seconds later, Pegasus's breathing had stopped.

"That's it," Scott said softly. "He's in a better place now."

Amy gasped, staring first at Pegasus and then up to Lou.

"It was the right choice, Amy," Lou said, tears streaming down her face. She put an arm around her sister. "It was the only choice. Now he'll be with Mom again."

In that moment, Amy suddenly realized how much

she needed her sister. "Oh, Lou," she sobbed against her shoulder. "I'm so glad you're here."

"And I always will be," Lou said softly. "I'll always be here for you, Amy, and you'll be here for me."

"Yes, Lou, always," Amy replied. "Always."

Chapter Ten

That night, Amy called Grandpa to tell him about Pegasus. At first, Grandpa wanted to return immediately.

"No, it's OK. Stay," she told him.

"But I feel so bad," he protested. "I should have been there."

"There wasn't anything you could have done," Amy replied. "There was nothing anyone could have done." The tears gathered in her throat, but she felt inwardly calm. She knew that she had done the right thing. Pegasus's suffering was over.

"And what about a burial?"

"Scott and Ty dug a grave in his favorite field," Amy said quietly. "And we planted an oak sapling beside it." She glanced out the kitchen window. It was getting dark now, but she could still make out the field and the slim young tree, silhouetted against the evening sky. "You don't have to come home early, Grandpa. We'll be OK."

"Well, I'll stay until next Sunday, then, like I planned," Grandpa said. "But if you need me, promise you'll call."

"I promise," Amy said. Then she launched into a new topic. "You wouldn't believe the idea Lou came up with to get more customers," Amy exclaimed.

Just then Lou came into the kitchen. "Is that Grandpa?" she asked.

Amy nodded. "Here's Lou, Grandpa. I'll let her tell you all about her idea," she said, handing over the phone.

As Lou spoke to Grandpa, telling him about the open house they were planning, Amy leaned against the sink and stared out at Pegasus's tree. She found it almost impossible to believe that he wasn't in his stall and that when she went out to feed the next morning he wouldn't be there. But looking up at the gray sky she knew that she had to accept it — Pegasus was gone and life had to move on. Still, there was something about the tree just being there that would keep Pegasus alive for her.

"It's all settled, then," Lou said, putting the phone down. "We're going to have the open house next Sunday — Marnie's last day. Grandpa thinks it's a great idea." She looked at Amy. "You know, this is going to be one busy week."

❧

Lou was right. There was a lot to be done — posters to be made, ads to be placed, food to be planned, and the final touches made to the stables. Marnie worked like crazy — she was so enthusiastic and really wanted the open house to be a huge success. Soraya and Matt helped as much as they could, and Amy found the days passing in a whirl of activity — going to school, helping with the open-house preparations, doing her normal chores, working Promise in the mornings and evenings. At night, when she fell into her bed, she was too exhausted to think, too tired even to dream.

On Thursday, Scott dropped by. Amy was sweeping the yard with Ty, Marnie was pruning the flowers in the hanging baskets, and Lou was attaching the nameplates to the horses' doors.

"Hi, guys," Scott called, as he was getting out of the car. "I just thought I'd stop by and see how you're getting along."

"We're doing fine," Lou said, going to meet him. "Almost ready for the big day."

"I've been spreading the word," Scott said. "So, I hope you're expecting a big crowd?"

"That's the plan," Lou said.

They stopped a few feet away from each other. "How are you?" Lou asked, her cheeks flushing slightly pink.

Amy and Marnie exchanged knowing looks.

"Fine," Scott replied to Lou. "Listen, do you need any help on Sunday? I'd be happy to lend a hand."

"Thanks," Lou said. "That would be really great." She smiled up at him.

There was a pause as they looked at each other. Suddenly seeming to become aware that they were being watched, Scott cleared his throat and turned to Amy. "So — how's it going with Promise?" he asked. "Have you made any progress?"

"You won't believe it!" Ty said, leaning on his broom.

"She's behaving herself?" Scott said to Amy.

Amy grinned at him. "You want to see?"

Getting Promise's halter, Amy led the palomino to the training ring on the longline, the saddle and bridle over her arm.

"What have you been doing with her?" Scott asked, opening the gate. "Lunging? Long-reining?"

"Riding," Amy replied, leading Promise into the ring. She grinned at his astonished face. "Watch."

She patted Promise and then vaulted lightly onto her, bareback. After riding the mare several times around the ring she halted.

"That's great," Scott said, looking impressed. He glanced at the tack. "What about with the saddle and bridle?"

"Oh, I can ride with those as well," Amy said. Her

voice was casual, but inwardly she was bubbling with delight.

Swinging her leg over Promise's back, she dismounted and got the saddle. She offered it to Promise to sniff, and when Promise had turned away, lifted it carefully onto the mare's golden back. The horse stood without moving as Amy did up the girth and then slipped on the bridle. Putting her foot in the stirrup, she mounted and rode in a circle.

"Well," she said, stopping Promise by the gate as the sweet sensation of success flowed through her, "what do you think?"

"Wow, that's amazing!" Scott exclaimed. He ran a hand through his hair. "How did you do it?"

"By listening," Amy said simply. "And respecting her."

"And she's OK for other people to ride?" Scott asked.

"She's getting there," Amy said. Only the day before, Promise had let Ty tack her up and ride her. She was still a little sensitive about the saddle being lifted near her, but with careful handling, Amy was sure that Promise would become less defensive and learn to trust other people as well.

"No one's going to believe this," Scott said, shaking his head. "Have you told Lisa yet?"

"I was going to call her tonight," Amy said.

"She'll be thrilled," Scott said. His blue eyes looked suddenly thoughtful. "You know, you should ask her permission to use Promise at the open house. People around here have heard of her. If they see that you've cured a supposedly rogue horse, they're bound to be impressed."

Amy thought for a moment. Why not? She knew Lou wanted her to do a display of joining up with a horse for the visitors to see. Why not use Promise, if Lisa Stillman thought it was OK? After all, it would have an impact on those people who had heard about the palomino, and if people hadn't, well, she was a very pretty, healthy horse and would look good in the ring. But she wouldn't do it unless Lisa agreed.

❧

After Scott had left, Amy phoned Fairfield. Lisa Stillman sounded astonished to hear that Promise was already ridable. "But you've only had her for a week!" she said. "And you're telling me she's cured?"

"Well, not completely," Amy replied. "But she's definitely improving. I can ride her and saddle her up, no problem. I just want her to get more confident with other people."

"But other stables had her for months at a time, and not one of them ever made a difference," Lisa Stillman said. "What on earth did you do?"

Amy told Lisa about her phone call to Eliza Chittick and about how Promise's behavior had changed when she had started trusting her and treating her with respect.

"This is amazing!" Lisa Stillman said as she listened to Amy's tale. "I have to see her!"

"Well, I was calling to ask if we could use Promise in a demonstration on Sunday. We're having an open house at Heartland." Amy explained the idea behind the day and how she needed a horse to join up with. "Promise would be ideal — if you'll give your permission, of course," she added politely.

"Sure, you can use her," Lisa Stillman said. "I'll even come along myself to see how she's doing. What time does it start?"

"Eleven o'clock," Amy said. "And the demonstration will be around twelve."

"I'll see you then," Lisa Stillman said.

Amy put the phone down, feeling excited but nervous. She knew that Ty was carefully preparing his talk about the alternative remedies they used at Heartland. His part of the demonstration was bound to go well. But the join up? It was normally such a private, intense experience. How would she feel doing it in front of a lot of strangers? What if it didn't work?

She pushed those thoughts away. It had to work. After all, Heartland's future depended on the demonstration being a success. And she would do *anything* to keep Heartland going. She had made a promise to Mom and a promise to herself.

❧

The final few days before the open house seemed to race by, but by quarter to eleven on Sunday morning Heartland was finally ready for the visitors to arrive. Amy, Lou, Marnie, Ty, and Soraya stood in the middle of the yard.

"We're ready!" Lou said, looking around in relief.

"And it's looking good!" Marnie said, gazing at the front stable block and the spotless yard.

"It sure is," Amy agreed. She looked at the horses that had their heads over their stall doors, their coats gleaming and their eyes shining. They all looked so healthy and happy. The hanging baskets provided a splash of cheerful color against the dark wood of the stables. Around the yard, Ty had put up signs to show visitors where to go. "It all looks so neat and clean!" Amy exclaimed.

"Well, everything except you!" Lou grinned.

Amy looked down at her filthy jeans. She had started work at five thirty that morning and hadn't had a second even to brush her hair. "I guess I'd better change," she admitted.

"Me, too," said Soraya.

They hurried upstairs to Amy's bedroom and changed

into jodhpurs and clean T-shirts. "I hope everything goes OK," Amy said, feeling butterflies starting to flutter in her stomach.

"It will," Soraya said, pulling her dark curls back into a ponytail. She glanced out the window. "We'd better hurry! I think the first people are arriving!"

They raced downstairs to find Ty directing a carload of visitors into the field they were using as a temporary parking lot. Just then, Scott's Jeep came up the drive. He stopped it near the house, and he and Matt jumped out.

"Hi, there!" Lou said, coming out of the house with a carton of sodas for the refreshments stall that Marnie was in charge of.

"Sorry we're late," Scott said. "I was called out first thing." He saw her with the big box and walked over. "Hey, do you want a hand?"

"Thanks," Lou said gratefully, letting him take the box from her. "There's a couple more cartons inside."

"No problem," Scott said. "I can take care of that."

"Hey, guys," Matt said, going over to Amy and Soraya. "What do you need me to do?"

"Could you take over the parking from Ty?" Amy suggested. "Soraya and I are going to show people around, and Ty's supposed to be giving out brochures and talking about what we do here."

"Sure. No problem," said Matt, jogging off.

The first group of visitors headed toward the yard.

Soraya glanced at Amy. "Well, here we go," she muttered as they drew closer. "Get ready to smile."

Amy nodded and, taking a deep breath, stepped forward. "Hi," she said brightly. "I'm Amy Fleming. Welcome to Heartland."

Soon the place was teeming with people. Although most of them were really friendly and interested in Heartland's work, there were some who clearly doubted the effectiveness of the methods used. Amy struggled to keep control of her frustration. She couldn't fathom how close-minded some people were.

"If one more person tells me that aromatherapy or herbal remedies won't work with horses, I'm going to scream," she muttered to Ty as she stopped to get some brochures from him.

Farther up the yard she could see Soraya telling a group of visitors the history of each horse.

"Relax," Ty said to her. He shrugged. "You know the folks around here. Not everyone's going to get it. We'll be lucky if we can convince a couple of people that our ways work."

But Amy couldn't think like that. She knew the methods they used at Heartland worked, and she desperately wanted *all* the visitors to realize that — to see what a unique and special place it really was.

"But why did they bother to come?" she demanded, thinking of a man she had talked to who refused to believe alternative remedies could have an effect. "Some of them just want to criticize."

"Yeah," Ty said easily. His eyes suddenly fixed on a point behind Amy's shoulder. "Speaking of which —"

Amy looked around. Ashley Grant was sauntering up the yard. Beside her was her mom, a tall, broad-shouldered woman with short blond hair.

"What are they doing here?" Amy hissed.

Val Grant caught sight of her and came over. "Hello, Amy," she said, her smile revealing a mouthful of perfect white teeth. "We thought we'd pop by and offer you our support."

Like that's true, Amy thought to herself. But she forced herself to smile back. "Thanks so much. It's nice to see you."

Val Grant's eyes flashed. "You've sure cleaned this place up."

"Hi, Ty," Ashley said, virtually ignoring Amy. She flicked her hair back. "How are you?"

"Fine." Ty coughed and started to shuffle the brochures.

"Can I have a brochure?" Ashley asked. Amy saw her gingerly take the sheet from Ty and smile.

Feeling a wave of irritation, she turned to excuse herself. "I'd better be going," she said to Val Grant. "There are so many people to see."

"Sure thing," Val Grant said. "We'll just have a look around. We're looking forward to seeing the demonstration later. Good luck." She laughed. At least her mouth did; her eyes stayed hard. "You never know, we may learn something."

Amy smiled briefly and then hurried away. Now, more than ever, she was determined that the join up would succeed.

🙞

At twelve o'clock, Scott, Lou, and Marnie started to encourage people to go to the schooling ring. Amy put Promise's saddle and bridle on the fence and then went to get the palomino.

"This is it, girl," she said, rubbing Promise's golden neck. "Please be good." Suddenly she realized that she hadn't seen Lisa Stillman. She felt a flash of disappointment but quickly pushed it down. There were more than enough people out there to impress.

She led Promise up to the training ring. At the sight of people clustered two deep around the fence, her stomach knotted with fear.

Ty had already started his talk.

To demonstrate the use of aromatherapy oils, Soraya led Sugarfoot into the ring, and Ty showed the crowd how the Shetland turned away from certain oils but sniffed long and hard at two of the bottles. "Horses know what will help them," he told the crowd. "Sugarfoot came to Heartland after his owner died. At that time, he liked the neroli oil; it helps with grief and depression. But now that he is getting better, he is drawn to the smells of bergamot and yarrow oils. Bergamot is an energizing oil, and yarrow relaxes. Sugarfoot's instincts help him choose the oils that will help him most."

Ty then started to work on the Shetland with T-touch circles and again pointed out to the audience how the Shetland moved himself to place certain parts of his head and body under his fingers.

Amy noticed the growing interest of the crowd as they began to murmur to one another.

"He's telling me how to help him," Ty told them. Leaving Sugarfoot he walked around the ring. "Horses try to communicate with us, but time after time humans just don't listen," he said. He looked around, and his dark eyes were serious and convincing. "Well, at Heartland we believe in listening. We don't whisper things to horses. We let *them* speak to *us*."

As he finished there was a burst of applause.

Promise started at the sudden noise. "It's OK," Amy quickly soothed her.

Soraya led Sugarfoot out of the ring, and Ty held up his hand for quiet. "Amy is now going to show you another way that we communicate with the horse. It is called the join up." There was another round of applause, and he walked over to the gate where Amy was waiting. He opened the gate. "It's all yours," he said to Amy. "Good luck."

Their eyes met.

Ty squeezed her shoulder. "Go on. You can do this. I know."

Taking a deep breath, Amy braced herself and led Promise into the ring.

The clapping died down and an expectant hush descended.

Horribly aware of the eyes watching her, Amy unclipped the lead rope and let Promise go. As the palomino trotted off around the ring, Amy heard a few murmurs and gasps from the people in the crowd who recognized Promise as Lisa Stillman's rogue horse. Amy knew she had to speak, to explain what she was doing, but for a moment her courage failed her. Suddenly she caught sight of Lou in the crowd. Her sister nodded and smiled at her, and Amy felt her confidence return.

"Promise is a horse that came to us with a behavior problem," she told the crowd. "For months she had been considered virtually unridable, refusing to be saddled or bridled. But then she came to Heartland. She has been here for two weeks, and her problem is pretty much cured — as I will show you at the end of this demonstration," she said, motioning to the saddle and bridle on the fence. "But first of all I will show you the technique we use to establish a relationship with a horse. Not a traditional relationship based on fear, but a relationship based on trust and understanding."

Moving to the center of the ring, she began.

The join up worked like a dream. Amy explained to the audience every signal that Promise gave. She could feel the tension in the crowd when she dropped her eyes and turned her back on the mare. And then she heard the universal gasp as Promise walked confidently over and rested her muzzle on Amy's shoulder. The audience's astonishment was obvious as she walked around the ring with the palomino following wherever she went.

To end the demonstration, Amy picked up the saddle and offered it to Promise. "I'm now asking her if I can saddle her up," she told the crowd. "By asking her permission I am showing that I respect her. Promise is a highly intelligent, proud horse — too proud to ever be bullied into obedience. She responds to respect, not reprimands."

After Promise had sniffed the saddle, Amy tacked her up, mounted, and then rode around the ring. She trotted the palomino in two serpentines and then cantered her in a perfect figure eight.

Drawing Promise to a halt in the middle of the ring, she dismounted. "In two weeks Promise has changed from an unridable rogue into the perfect pleasure horse." She smiled at the crowd. "And it's all because, here at Heartland, we listen to the horse."

The applause broke out. It went on and on. Patting Promise, Amy smiled happily. They had done it! She and Promise had shown them all!

Ty came back into the ring. "So, are there any questions?"

There was a murmur in the crowd, and then a man raised his hand. It was the same man Amy had been talking to earlier who seemed determined to believe that Heartland's methods would never work.

"How do we know that the horse really was unridable?" he demanded. "We only have your word for it."

"You're right," Ty replied. "But there are enough people here who know or who have heard of this horse to back us up. Ask your neighbors."

Amy heard the crowd murmur an assent. But then she noticed movement near the gate.

"It's my belief that horse was drugged!" The voice was loud and strident. Amy swung around to see Val Grant pushing her way to the front of the fence. "It's the oldest trick in the book," the blond woman announced. "Get a rogue horse, sedate it, and then make it look like you've worked a miracle. If you come back tomorrow, I think you'll see a very different horse."

To Amy's horror, people in the crowd started to nod. "That's not true!" she exclaimed. "I'd never drug a horse."

"Well, of course you'd say that," the first man spoke up again. "You want our business."

"Not if it means drugging a horse!" Amy said. "That's against everything Heartland stands for."

Val Grant spoke up again. "Well, these people just don't seem to believe you."

"I believe you." The crowd turned. A woman pushed open the gate and walked into the ring. With her long blond hair and elegant jodhpurs, Lisa Stillman was instantly recognizable to all who followed the show circuit.

"Lisa!" Amy gasped.

Lisa Stillman walked to the center of the ring. "What some of you may not realize," she explained, "is that this horse is one of mine. I can vouch for the fact that she was as unridable as Amy Fleming says. Although," she shot caustic looks at the man who had spoken out and at Val Grant, "you may of course choose to doubt my word as well." She looked around at the rest of the audience. "The fact is, it's true. This was the horse's last chance, and as far as I'm concerned Heartland has worked nothing less than a miracle. She isn't drugged, anyone can see that by looking into her eyes." She patted Promise. "When I first agreed to let Promise come here, I was as skeptical as many of you," she announced. "But not anymore. After what I've seen, I realize that this is the way of the future. From now on," Lisa turned and smiled at Amy, "any problem horse of mine will be coming to Heartland."

"Thank you!" Amy gasped.

"And now," Lisa Stillman said, "I think we should give our hosts a round of applause."

This time the applause was deafening. People clapped their hands and whistled. Sensing Promise tense up, Amy quickly led her away from the noisy ring and back to the peaceful sanctuary of her stall.

"Thank you," she whispered to the mare.

Promise snorted and nuzzled her shoulder.

Suddenly the stall door flew open. It was Matt and Soraya. "That was fantastic!" Soraya gasped.

"The way that Lisa Stillman just marched into the ring was so cool!" Matt almost shouted.

"Val Grant didn't know what to do!" Soraya grinned. "We saw her storming back to her car with Ashley, looking really angry." She hugged Amy. "And you were great! You seemed so cool and confident."

Amy grinned. "I was terrified!"

"You should see all the people by the ring now," Matt said. "Everyone's trying to talk to Lou and Ty about bringing their horses here. You're going to have so much business. You're going to have a waiting list."

Amy could hardly believe it, but when she returned to the ring with Soraya and Matt, it was clear they were right. People were crowding around Lou and Ty. Amy's eyes widened. It was wonderful, just what they'd wanted, but how were they ever going to cope with the extra work?

Her sister suddenly spotted her. "Amy!" she called, waving.

Amy made her way through the crowd, with people patting her on the back and congratulating her. "Hi!" she exclaimed, reaching Lou. "Isn't this amazing?"

"Yeah," Lou said. "Look at this!" She waved a piece of paper under Amy's nose that was filled with names and addresses. "And Ty has more. After today we'll be able to fill the barns three times over."

"How will we deal with it all?" Amy cried, half in delight, half in despair.

"That's the best part of all," Lou said. "Lisa Stillman asked if we'll take her nephew Ben as a stable hand. She wants him to learn everything we do so that he can return to her barn and practice the same therapies we use. Even better, she's going to pay us to train him!"

"I can't believe it, Lou!" Amy gasped, flinging her arms around her sister's neck. "It's going to be so much better."

Lou hugged her back joyfully.

"I know you said you'd have wild parties when I was gone," a much-loved voice said behind them. "But isn't this a bit much?"

Amy and Lou turned. "Grandpa!" they both cried in delight.

Jack Bartlett smiled at them. "Yes," he said, "I'm home."

℞

That evening, after the horses had been fed and the yard cleared, Amy walked down the drive to Pegasus's favorite field. The air was still and peaceful. Amy leaned over the wooden gate and watched the shadows lengthening across the grass.

Ty, Soraya, Matt, and Scott had gone home, and Marnie was in her bedroom, packing for her trip back to the city the next day. Amy knew she was going to miss her. After all, it was Marnie who had helped her realize that she had to run Heartland in her own way and follow her own instincts, and that she and Lou had to work together as a team.

A cool breeze shivered across Amy's skin. After the commotion of the open house, everything seemed twice as quiet. It had been a wonderful day. For the moment, at least, Heartland's financial worries were over, and with Ben Stillman as an additional stable hand there would be more time to spend with the horses. *Maybe I'll even get a chance to enter some jumping classes,* Amy thought.

She looked at the freshly planted oak tree and her heart twisted. There was just one thing missing from her life — Pegasus.

"Why did you have to go?" she whispered painfully.

But even as she spoke, she knew the answer. Life moves on. Nothing lasts forever.

The light faded and the evening shadows covered the tree. A last, lone bird sang out.

"Amy?"

She looked around. Grandpa and Lou were walking toward her through the October dusk.

"We saw you from the kitchen window," Lou said.

"May we join you?" Grandpa asked quietly.

Amy nodded her head.

For a moment all three of them stood by the gate in silence. "Today was a good day," Lou said at last.

"Yeah," Amy said. "It was."

Grandpa put a hand lightly on their shoulders. "I think tomorrow will be a good day, too," he said. "I'm proud of you, and your mom would have been proud, too. Now Heartland has a future, and you've made it your own."

Amy looked at her Grandpa and at Lou, and then her gaze fell on the slender young oak. Life was about the future, not about clinging to the past. Staring at the tree, her lips moved silently. *"Good-bye, Pegasus."*

Despite the shadows of the night, the bird sang on.

Heartland™

healing horses, healing hearts.

Unbridle the Power of Heartland...